"I can tell you exactly me…"

Zoe set one hand on her hip. "You can walk right out of here and never bother me again."

Ryan's instincts warned him that he should do as she suggested and never see her again. But his blood pulsed hot and fast through his veins, setting his entire body alight.

Indulging his desire for her would be madness.

"You're right when you say it would be better if I left and never came back," he said, cursing the insistent thrum of hunger that made him reach out and snag her waist, drawing her toward him. "But that doesn't stop me from wanting to do this."

Ryan wrapped his arm a little tighter about her, drawing her slim curves more firmly into contact with his unyielding planes, and, to his delight, her lips parted on a soft moan. This was his cue and he dipped his head, sealing his lips to hers.

Time didn't just slow. It stopped. Her lips parted on a luxurious sigh, granting him access to her sweet mouth while her body molded to his.

Rushing this first kiss would be a crime. Instead, he intended to savor every slow, sexy second of it…

* * *

Revenge with Benefits is part of the Sweet Tea and Scandal series from Cat Schield.

Dear Reader,

It's always bittersweet when I finish the last book in a series, especially when I love the characters. But while *Revenge with Benefits* is the final book in my Sweet Tea and Scandal trilogy, there are lots of scandalous Charleston stories that need to be told.

Revenge with Benefits is my twenty-fifth Harlequin Desire. As I look back on all the books I've written, I can't believe how fast the time has gone and what an amazing journey it has been bringing the stories of my heart to readers around the world. Thank you for being there with me through all the romantic ups and downs as my characters find their happily-ever-afters.

Happy reading,

Cat Schield

CAT SCHIELD

—

REVENGE WITH BENEFITS

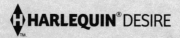

Recycling programs
for this product may
not exist in your area.

ISBN-13: 978-1-335-60347-0

Revenge with Benefits

Copyright © 2019 by Catherine Schield

This edition published by arrangement with Harlequin Books S.A.

For questions and comments about the quality of this book,
please contact us at CustomerService@Harlequin.com.

Printed in U.S.A.

Cat Schield has been reading and writing romance since high school. Although she graduated from college with a BA in business, her idea of a perfect career was writing books for Harlequin. And now, after winning the Romance Writers of America 2010 Golden Heart® Award for Best Contemporary Series Romance, that dream has come true. Cat lives in Minnesota with her daughter, Emily, and their Burmese cat. When she's not writing sexy, romantic stories for Harlequin Desire, she can be found sailing with friends on the St. Croix River, or in more exotic locales, like the Caribbean and Europe. She loves to hear from readers. Find her at catschield.net and follow her on Twitter, @catschield.

Books by Cat Schield

Harlequin Desire

Las Vegas Nights

At Odds with the Heiress
A Merger by Marriage
A Taste of Temptation
The Black Sheep's Secret Child
Little Secret, Red Hot Scandal
The Heir Affair

Sweet Tea and Scandal

Upstairs Downstairs Baby
Substitute Seduction
Revenge with Benefits

Visit her Author Profile page at Harlequin.com, or catschield.net, for more titles.

Prologue

While the keynote speaker for the Beautiful Women Taking Charge event droned on, Everly Briggs contemplated Zoe Crosby and recognized the former Charleston, South Carolina trophy wife was the weak link in her plan.

Before the networking function Everly had researched the attendees and settled on two women recently wronged by the men in their lives. Over cocktails, Everly had chatted up both women, sharing her own tale of how her sister had been wronged by wealthy entrepreneur Ryan Dailey. In addition to Zoe Crosby, she'd encouraged London McCaffrey to pour out her heartbreak after Linc Thurston broke off their engagement.

"We've each been the victim of a wealthy, powerful man," Everly said, thinking that was most true of Zoe. Her ex-husband had hired Charleston's most ruthless divorce attorney and rumor had it that Zoe's settlement was going to be eaten up by her lawyer's fees. "Don't you think it's time we get a little payback?"

"Anything we try would only end up making things worse for us," Zoe said, her hesitation grating on Everly's nerves.

Up until this moment, Zoe Crosby had been listening and nodding sympathetically. Before meeting her, Everly figured if anyone would want to take down a powerful man it would be a wife who'd been cheated on by one, then cast aside and forced to defend her honor in divorce court.

Instead, Everly was starting to understand why Tristan Crosby had treated his wife with such disdain. The woman was too soft, too passive. She lacked fire and purpose. Well, Everly would just have to stir up the socialite's indignation over how she'd been treated and drive Zoe into the revenge scheme.

"Not if we go after each other's men," Everly explained, gratified to see London McCaffrey nodding in understanding. Zoe still looked worried, so Everly continued to lay out her plan. "Think about it," she said, fighting to keep impatience out of her voice. "We're strangers at a cocktail party. Who would ever connect us? I go after Linc. London goes after Tristan and, Zoe, you go after Ryan."

"When you say 'go after,'" Zoe said cautiously, "what do you have in mind?"

Everly resisted the urge to roll her eyes. From the first she'd suspected Zoe would be too timid to make a good revenge partner, but at least the socialite could be manipulated into doing as Everly wanted.

"In Ryan's case, his sister is running for state senate," Everly said, deciding she'd better monitor Zoe's part of the plan to make sure Ryan Dailey paid dearly for putting her sister in jail.

After all, he was responsible for breaking Kelly's heart and driving her to act out against his firm by deleting millions of dollars worth of engineering drawings. If he hadn't led her sister on, Everly was convinced Kelly never would've snapped like that.

Zoe's frown deepened at Everly's suggestion that she go after Ryan indirectly. "I thought we were supposed to be going after the men. I don't feel comfortable."

"Since Ryan destroyed my sister's life," Everly explained with elaborate patience even as her irritation reached a boiling point, "it only seems fair that we ruin his sister's chances at being elected." Her pause was too brief to give Zoe a chance to argue further. "Getting at Ryan through his sister is the best way to go. Okay?"

Zoe's abbreviated nod didn't fill Everly with confidence. Well, if the socialite couldn't do what needed to be done, Everly would just have to take care of things herself.

One

Fingers biting into the armrest of the hair salon's cheap vinyl chair, Zoe Crosby—*Alston*, she reminded herself yet again—stared at her reflection. As of today it was official. Forevermore she would check the *divorced* box on every survey form or application that asked her marital status. Even though for the last year she'd told herself it wasn't her fault, the shame of failure sent heat rushing over her skin, leaving her feeling sweaty and miserable.

"Are you sure about this?" the stylist asked, her face screwed into doubtful lines. Penny raked her fingers through Zoe's long, silky hair. "Your hair is so gorgeous. The caramel color with the paler blond streaks. Are you sure you don't want me to take an inch off and call it good?"

Zoe set her jaw and shook her head. "No. I want you to shave it all off."

The stylist looked even more pained, if that was possible. "It's none of my business, and you are beautiful enough to wear your hair whatever length you want, but I wouldn't be doing my job if I didn't talk you out of doing something that radical."

Tristan had been very particular about her hair. He'd wanted it to end exactly at her nipples, deeming it the perfect length. She was not allowed to have bangs or layers. Just a silky, straight curtain with blunt ends. She hadn't been allowed to curl it or to put it up when he'd been around. It was just one of the many ways he'd controlled her.

Zoe sighed, her courage deflating. She'd marched into the hair salon after deciding to shave her head as a middle finger salute to her ex. Tristan couldn't control her anymore and that was empowering, but maybe getting rid of all her hair was a bit extreme. Still, she needed to do something to mark the day that she was utterly and joyfully free of Tristan Crosby. Her gaze swept the photos of women modeling various haircuts lining the walls, snagging on one in particular.

"What about that?" She pointed to a brunette sporting a short, spiky cut. "Only I'd like to go platinum blond."

The stylist looked relieved. "With your bone structure, that look would be fantastic on you."

"Do it."

An hour and a half later Zoe regarded her reflection and didn't recognize herself. Gone was the traditional wife of a successful Charleston businessman with her sweater sets and pretty floral dresses. In her place was an edgy replacement in a graphic T-shirt and torn black jeans. Zoe shivered as she raked her fingers through her new do.

Tristan would hate her dramatic transformation.

But then dismay flooded her. When would she stop running all her decisions through the filter of pleasing her ex-husband? All the more reason to make the change. She needed to think about what made *her* happy.

Plus, she had another reason for altering her appearance.

With step one of her transformation complete, Zoe exited the salon and popped into a drugstore to purchase lipstick and an eye shadow kit in smoky shades that Tristan Crosby's ex-wife would never have been allowed to wear. In the parking lot, she sat in her car and applied the makeup.

Drawing confidence from her new look, Zoe put her car in gear and headed to the campaign headquarters for Susannah Dailey-Kirby's state senate race. She intended to volunteer for the campaign, making herself indispensable and gathering as much dirt as she could to take down Ryan Dailey's twin.

Everly had suggested the strategy to get back at him for Everly's sister, Kelly.

At the time Zoe had been happy for the input. She'd had absolutely no idea how one went about seeking revenge. Her time married to Tristan had been all about surviving his psychological battery, leaving her little energy for schemes or the gumption to carry them out.

Yet that wasn't completely true. As a safety net, she'd managed to siphon off tens of thousands of dollars from her allowance during her marriage. Having grown up not exactly poor but with a family that lived paycheck to paycheck, she'd liked the idea of financial independence that ready access to the secret stash offered her.

She should have realized Tristan would view any attempt at self-sufficiency as a threat to his power. When he'd found out, he'd reclaimed her stash and monitored her spending more closely. But instead of intimidating her, his actions had made her more determined, and less trusting of her so-called friends and allies.

The crushing loneliness of being married to Tristan was almost as bad as the emotional and psychological abuse he'd heaped on her. Maybe she shouldn't have let Tristan convince her to quit college after her junior year. But she'd chosen to plan an elaborate wedding instead of finishing her degree. Floating down the aisle mere months before her twenty-first birthday, she'd actually believed the rest of her life would be like a fairy tale. And in some ways it had. Only she hadn't been the lucky princess rescued by Prince Charming. Tristan had turned out to be more like the evil king who overtaxed the peasants and punished his subjects whenever the mood struck him.

She'd had no real friends, as was glaringly obvious in the wake of her separation from Tristan and subsequent divorce. No one had stepped up to support or to help her. She'd become a pariah in their tight social circles as Tristan had leaked false stories of her infidelity. No one had cared or believed her when she'd denied the allegations. It was one thing if a man strayed, but unseemly for a Southern woman.

Zoe came out of her reverie as she neared North Charleston. Susannah Dailey-Kirby's campaign headquarters wasn't far from the humane society where Zoe volunteered once a week, loving the time she got to spend with the animals. She'd grown up with dogs and cats, but Tristan had refused to allow her to have a pet.

After parking her car in the strip mall parking lot, Zoe strode along the sidewalk in the direction of the campaign's storefront. For the last week or so she'd been sitting at the fast-food franchise across the street, contemplating the comings and goings of the staff and gathering courage to make her approach. In the weeks since she'd agreed to the revenge bargain, her enthusiasm for the project had waned.

But she'd made a promise and staying true to her commitments was an intrinsic element of her personality she couldn't just set aside. She couldn't help it, even when that trait had kept her in a bad marriage past all self-preservation. She'd meant it when she'd stood before family and friends and pledged to love, honor and cherish Tristan until death. That he'd done everything to destroy her good intentions hadn't lessened her dedication to her vows. No doubt she'd still be married and miserable if he hadn't decided to cast her aside.

Some days it was hard for her to distinguish whether the brunt of her anger over the failure of her marriage was directed at Tristan or herself. The rational part of her mind blamed Tristan's unreasonable expectations, but her emotions turned the fault on her shortcomings.

Approaching the campaign headquarters, Zoe took a deep breath and held it while she pushed all doubts and worries out of her mind. She needed to focus on the task at hand or everything would be lost.

She'd decided to keep her backstory vague, because she didn't want to talk about her ex-husband or the messy divorce he'd put her through. She was restarting her life as Zoe Alston and that opened up a whole range of possibilities. But first she had to see her commitment through.

Gathering a deep breath for courage, Zoe pushed through the front door, expecting the campaign office to be buzzing despite the election being a year off. But the space she entered was static and tense, as if she'd burst onto the scene of a tragedy.

A tiny bell had rung as she'd entered, but no one had noticed. The same chime sounded now as the door swung shut behind her. The campaign staff remained focused on a large TV. Feeling like an intruder, she advanced two steps into the room and then hesitated, unsure if she should continue or retreat. She'd obviously stumbled into something dire.

Four people stood in a semicircle surrounding a tall, slender man with thick, neatly combed gray hair. Phones rang at several desks but no one paid them any heed. In fact, the staffers' only reaction was to dial the TV volume up.

Zoe shifted her focus from the campaign workers to the news footage that held their attention. It took her a couple of seconds to realize that someone new had en-

tered the race and apparently this was very bad indeed.
Realizing this was not a good time for her to approach
the campaign team about volunteering, she started to
pivot back the way she'd come and promptly collided
with someone.

Like the campaign staff, she'd been so focused on the
television coverage she hadn't noticed the tinkling bell.
Now, however, as her nose took a hit from the man's co-
logne, her senses went on full alert. She was still reeling
from the masculine scent of him as her right shoulder
impacted with his rock-solid chest. It was like hitting
a wall. Zoe bounced off him like a kitten off a mastiff.

She stumbled and might've fallen had he not caught
her by the arm. His fingers were strong. His grip firm
and steadying. It sent her heart sprinting as he guided her
back the way she'd come. Her brain struggled to catch
up with the to-and-fro movements of her body and de-
code the electric jolt she felt when he'd first touched her.

Her gaze collided with pale gray eyes of incredible
intensity. For a moment she was utterly mesmerized.
And then recognition flared. She gulped in panic.

Ryan Dailey.

Less than thirty seconds had passed since she'd initiated her part of the revenge plot and already she'd
bumped into her target. And what an unexpected encounter it was shaping up to be.

The man's sharp jawline, hawkish gaze, impossibly
wide shoulders and sensual grin packed a solid wallop.
Tingles raced across her nerve endings as heat built
beneath her skin. It raced past her throat and exploded
in her cheeks.

"You okay?" Ryan Dailey asked, his deep, rich voice rumbling against her eardrums and awakening queer flutters in her stomach.

"Yeah." It was all she could manage.

"I'm Ryan Dailey," he said, letting his focus flow over her white-blond spikes, dark plum lips and edgy bohemian outfit. "Susannah's brother."

While he checked her out, she took in his custom navy suit, white shirt and pale blue tie. Even with the four-inch heels on her ankle boots making her about five-nine, the man towered over her. Yet despite his imposing stature, she didn't experience the bitter taste of anxiety her ex-husband had often awakened.

But that didn't mean she felt calm.

"I'm Zoe…" Her mind froze before she could add her last name. For eight years she'd gone by Zoe Crosby. Those days were done.

"Nice to meet you, Zoe," Ryan said, smoothly filling in the awkward gap. The way his gray eyes sharpened with interest, he seemed to mean it.

"Nice to meet you, too." She couldn't seem to peel her gaze free, but had enough presence of mind to lift her elbow and alert him that she no longer needed his continued support.

His steely fingers relaxed and slid away, but her skin prickled beneath her black leather jacket as she continued to react to the pressure of his touch.

"You're new to Susannah's campaign," he remarked.

"What makes you say that?"

"If you'd been around before, I would've noticed you."

His comment reawakened those anxious flutters in

her stomach. The interest in his eyes was a little too keen, so Zoe settled deeper into playing her role of eager volunteer with nothing to hide.

"I'm really interested in volunteering for the campaign, but it seems like today might not be the best day to be here." She indicated the cluster of staff and then glanced toward the front door. "They seem really busy. Maybe I'll come back another time."

"Don't go." His cajoling smile sent a lance of delight through her. "Come on. I'll introduce you."

Zoe found herself smiling in return. "How about I wait right here and if they have time, you wave me over."

Offering her a brief nod, he moved past her.

Zoe stared after him, appalled and thrilled in turns. That was Ryan Dailey?

Despite her promise to stay, she slipped out the front door, sucking in a huge breath of air as she escaped the charged atmosphere. No wonder Everly had suggested Zoe focus on the sister. Taking down such a formidable man would've been beyond Zoe's abilities even if she hadn't been brought low by her ex-husband's cold-blooded machinations.

Yet, Ryan Dailey wasn't Tristan. He didn't seem the sort who took pleasure in being ruthless. That didn't mean he wasn't dangerous, especially given what had happened to Everly's sister, but Zoe didn't sense she was in peril.

At least not yet.

Interesting, Ryan mused. Bumping into her had stirred something that had been missing from his life for a long time. Lust. When was the last time he'd noticed a woman and wanted to put his mark on her? To take her to bed and satisfy a basic physical need, indulge in a whole host of dirty fantasies?

The chemistry between them had shivered across his nerve endings and rattled his bones. As he headed to the back of the office, he continued to be aware of her presence. He rubbed his chest where her shoulder had struck him. The spot seemed to buzz in the aftermath of the contact. In fact, the collision had started a chain reaction through his body.

But the uptick in Ryan's mood faded fast as he approached the campaign staffers huddled in front of the TV. The news segment on Lyle Abernathy entering the state senate race was over, but the strategizing about how to handle things was just getting started.

Ryan joined the group, noting Gil Moore's grim expression. "Hi, Gil."

"Hey, Ryan. I take it you heard."

"About Abernathy? Yeah."

"It's going to be bad," the campaign manager said.

"How's Susannah doing?"

"You know her motto. Never let them see you sweat."

Ryan acknowledged Gil's words with a nod. "Someone is here to volunteer. Her name is…" Ryan turned to where he'd left Zoe standing only to discover she'd gone. "Damn it."

He couldn't believe he was panicking. It spoke to the strong effect she had on him. Now that she'd bolted, he couldn't bear the thought that he'd never see her again.

"Looks like she took off."

"She didn't think her timing was right."

"Hopefully we haven't scared her off for good," Gil said. "Did you get a name?"

"Zoe." It wasn't much. Definitely not enough to track her down. "If she comes back, can you let me know? She has really short blond hair and a black leather jacket. Sort of a bohemian style."

Gil nodded. "We'll keep a lookout."

"Thanks." Ryan was grateful the campaign manager didn't ask any more questions. "I'd better go find out how Susannah's doing."

He headed towards his twin sister's office near the back of the building. On entering, he found her seated at her desk, staring at her computer. Her long black hair lay in a sleek curtain against her royal blue suit. Her beautiful face was relaxed; she looked not the least bit flustered that her campaign had just gotten that much harder.

Susannah looked up, her gray eyes narrowing. "What are you doing here?"

"I came to see if you're okay." Ryan knew it was a useless gesture as soon as he spoke. Still, he didn't regret rushing over. It had enabled him to meet Zoe.

"Oh, for heaven's sake! You and Mom. I just got off the phone with her a few minutes ago. I'm fine." And she meant it. Even when they were kids nothing had seemed to faze Susannah. Her unflappability would serve her well in the months to come. "Lyle is barely more than a speed bump."

Ryan glanced over his shoulder to where her staff

had fallen to conversing in low tones among themselves. "Gil doesn't seem to share your opinion."

"He likes to worry."

"You don't worry enough."

"What good would it do me?" Susannah asked, her brows coming together. "Lyle switched districts because he wasn't going to get elected to a fourth term, and he's too arrogant to believe that I won't be as much competition as Jeb Harrell."

"It's your first shot at running for state senate."

And you're a woman. Ryan knew better than to add the second part. Abernathy would throw dirt at Susannah any way he could. It was a sure bet he would use her gender against her.

"I'm a fantastic candidate for this district and everyone knows it." She paused and gave him a cocky little smile. "Including Lyle Abernathy."

"That'll just make him play dirty."

"I'm as squeaky clean as it gets," his twin reminded him. Then, seeing Ryan's continued doubt, she huffed impatiently. "There's nothing for him to use against me."

"That won't stop him. He'll make stuff up."

"We'll be ready."

Ryan opened his mouth to argue but decided he'd be wasting his breath. Susannah Dailey-Kirby was not a woman in need of his assistance.

The walls separating Susannah's office from the rest of the campaign headquarters were made of glass. Blinds had been added in case she needed privacy, but at the moment they were open. Ryan caught himself glancing a third time toward the front door where he'd last glimpsed Zoe.

Susannah followed the direction of his gaze. "Looking for something?"

"Someone. Your newest volunteer."

"I don't see anyone."

"With everything going on, she left before anyone met her. I was hoping she'd changed her mind and come back."

"My," his sister drawled, "she must've been something for you to be this interested. Was she pretty?"

"Yes."

Was he crazy to be so preoccupied with a woman he'd talked to for less than a minute? But then he remembered how bumping into her had short-circuited his system and knocked all thoughts of politics and Lyle Abernathy from his mind.

"Very pretty?"

"Very pretty. But she was different from the women I'm usually attracted to."

"How so?"

For a second Ryan wondered if he could put into words his unexpected reaction. He met hundreds of women a year. Why this particular one? While beautiful, she wasn't the most stunning woman he'd ever met and he hadn't spoken with her long enough to determine if she was bright or funny. Yet her impact on him lingered.

"She dressed like a badass. Black jeans and a graphic tee. Spiky blond hair and dark makeup. Sort of a 'flower child meets rock-and-roll' vibe." Yet beneath the tough-girl exterior he'd sensed her vulnerability.

"Seriously?" His sister made no attempt to hide her amusement. "You're right. That doesn't sound like your type at all."

He was tired of dating successful, sophisticated women like his sister—women who made it their mission to kick the world's ass. He wanted someone who could use his help. A woman who wasn't afraid to need him. "Maybe what I need is someone totally different."

Despite his mistakes with Kelly Briggs, Ryan liked the idea of being someone's hero and he refused to shy away from the arrogance of being convinced he was right when he acted in another person's best interest. Sure, maybe in this day and age women didn't want to be rescued or helped. Maybe they demanded the power in their relationships be balanced and equal. Ryan wasn't opposed to that, but what was wrong with letting their guard down and letting a guy flex his muscles once in a while?

Zoe intrigued him. He'd glimpsed something in her eyes that triggered his protective instincts. Which might prove problematic, given what had happened when he'd tried to help Kelly Briggs. She'd misinterpreted his assistance as some deep emotional connection between them. When he'd explained his concern was strictly platonic, she'd struck out against his company in a vicious act of revenge.

"But this isn't about me," Ryan objected. "It's about your campaign. You need all the help you can get. Especially now that Lyle has joined the race."

"Sure." His sister gave him a wry smile. "You keep telling yourself that. I hope she comes back." Susannah's eyes twinkled. "For the campaign's sake, of course." She paused to let her ribbing sink in and then added, "What did you say her name was?"

"Zoe. Hopefully she'll come back."

"If she does, we'll make sure we get all her details. I don't want her to disappear on you a second time."

Ryan opened his mouth to deny his interest and sighed instead. "That would be great. I have to get going. Call me if anything new comes up."

Before he could go, Susannah caught his arm. "I love you, big brother. Thanks for worrying about me even if I don't really need it."

He covered her hand with his. "It's what I do."

"I know. And I worry about you in turn." She spoke in a low tone. "I hope your mystery woman comes back and that she's great because you deserve someone fabulous in your life."

"I'm fine," he said automatically.

"Of course you're fine," she countered. "But I want you to be fantastic and the right woman could do that for you."

Susannah had married the first man she'd ever dated and they lived the blissful life of the perfect couple. She and Jefferson had been married for ten years and had two beautiful children, Violet and Casey, ages six and eight. In addition to being a supportive wife and supermom, she was a corporate attorney with the top law firm in the city. Every day she strove to take successful to new levels and did it with grace and ease.

"Jeff is a lucky man to have you," Ryan said. "I'm

afraid you might have set the bar too high for my future wife."

With a quick wave of her hand, Susannah dismissed his compliment. "We're a great team. I couldn't do any of this without him."

While Ryan wondered if that was true, he gave her a hard hug and took his leave.

Despite his sister's confidence that she could handle whatever trash Lyle threw at her in the senate race, Ryan didn't like this new development. It was time for him to pay his buddy downtown a visit. He might have a fresh take on what sort of dirty tricks they could expect in the months between now and election day.

Two

The day after Zoe's first attempt to join Susannah Dailey-Kirby's state senate campaign, she returned to the storefront, hoping for less chaos and no Ryan. Although the atmosphere continued to buzz with activity and anticipation, the staffers were no longer in crisis mode. She was greeted as soon as the door closed behind her.

"Hi, I'm Tonya." A pretty redhead in her midtwenties wearing jeans and a T-shirt emblazoned with Dailey for Senate approached Zoe. "Is there something I can do to help you?"

"Yes, I was here yesterday and—"

Tanya interrupted her. "Are you Zoe?"

That the staffer knew her name sent a shock through Zoe. Had she been found out already? Impossible.

"Yes."

"Wonderful. We're so glad you came back. Ryan mentioned that you'd stopped by but left before we could get any of your information."

"You all looked really busy," Zoe said, hoping her relief didn't show. "I just thought I'd try a different time."

"Well, we're really glad you did. Have you ever volunteered for a political campaign before?"

Zoe shook her head and Tonya began to describe the various activities volunteers could participate in.

"Why don't you come sit at my desk and I'll get some basic information from you."

While it was easy for Zoe to give Tonya her email and phone number, when it came to her home address, she was cagier. "I'm crashing with a friend at the moment. Can I give you a PO Box?"

Tonya looked doubtful but nodded. "I guess that would be okay. Are you looking for a permanent place?"

"That's the plan." Zoe pictured her cot in the back room of the retail space she'd rented a year earlier. That was before legal fees had consumed her divorce settlement and jeopardized her dream of running a consignment store that helped victims of domestic violence get back on their feet financially. "I just need something I can afford."

"Sure." Tonya went on to ask questions about what sort of work Zoe did and what she saw herself doing for the campaign.

While Zoe answered Tonya's questions, her gaze was drawn toward the large glassed-in office at the back of the campaign headquarters. From this angle, Zoe could

see Susannah working on her computer. Zoe's gut tightened. She was dreading her first meeting with Susannah, knowing she was going to do everything she could
to cause the woman harm.

Guilt gouged her conscience. She'd been so focused
on getting through her divorce and being angry at everything Tristan had done to her that she'd barely considered the damage her bargain with London and Everly
would do to an innocent third party. Zoe gave herself
a mental shake. She couldn't start thinking like this or
she'd never be able to go through with what she planned.
Instead, she focused on Everly's justification that Ryan
deserved to feel the sort of pain and frustration Everly
had gone through because of what he'd done to her
sister.

While she shied away from dwelling on the ethics of
what she and her coconspirators were up to, Zoe heard
the front door open behind her and noted how the energy in the room ratcheted up several notches. Tonya's
attention shifted past Zoe and her expression relaxed
into a relieved half smile. Alarm bells began to ring in
Zoe's mind. Had she been found out? Was someone
coming to haul her away? She balled her hands in her
lap and dug her fingernails into her palms to fight down
panic. Letting her imagination run amok wasn't going
to make her job any easier.

"Hi, Ryan," Tonya said, her smile turning supernova.
"How are you doing today?"

Learning that Ryan was the person who'd just arrived didn't calm Zoe's nerves at all. She'd bolted after
meeting him the day before, determining she was too

rattled by her sharp reaction to their brief encounter to stick around and pretend she was just an average campaign volunteer.

Now, feeling Ryan's approach in a rush of tingles over her skin, Zoe contemplated the younger woman and realized that Tonya had a crush on the handsome businessman. This gave Zoe a little breathing room. At least all eyes wouldn't be on her for now.

"I'm great," Ryan said in his velvet voice. "How are you doing, Tonya?"

The woman rolled her eyes significantly. "Way better than yesterday. The news about Lyle was such a shock. But of course Susannah calmed everyone down. She's so amazing."

The hero worship in Tanya's eyes might have amused Zoe if her own heart wasn't pounding so hard in reaction to Ryan Dailey.

"She is that," Ryan agreed as he stepped into Zoe's line of sight. "You came back," he said, a warm smile curving his sculpted lips. "That's great."

Zoe's gaze drifted upward over his light gray suit, white shirt and peach-colored tie. Her mouth was practically watering by the time she noted the faint stubble on his chin that gave him a slightly rakish air.

While preparing to take down Ryan Dailey, Zoe had done extensive online research. Despite his wealth and business success, the man wasn't much for stepping into the public eye. She'd had only the headshot of him on his company's web site to recognize him by. That photo hadn't prepared her for the man's compelling presence.

By contrast, his sister enjoyed being in the spotlight.

She was on the board of several charities focused on children's issues. With her husband at her side, she attended all sorts of events. Although Zoe had seen her many times over the years, they ran in completely different circles and never crossed paths. Zoe couldn't imagine what she could possibly say to engage such a brilliant, successful lawyer.

Whatever interests Ryan Dailey pursued in his personal life, he kept a tight lid on his activities. Zoe had found no trace of his love life in the media, but she suspected like so many wealthy and powerful men, he liked arm candy. Beautiful and sexy women that were meant to be showed off. They accentuated a man's virility.

But Ryan Dailey didn't need help in that department.

Zoe cursed as she noted her breathlessness. "Everyone seemed really busy yesterday," she explained.

"I'm glad you came back."

The fact that he sounded sincere combined with the keen interest in his gray eyes sent a shiver of awareness through her.

To Zoe's dismay, she recognized what lay beneath the shrilling of her nerves: attraction. It sizzled through her like lightning, awakening a fever she'd never known with her husband. Their marriage hadn't been a love match. He'd chosen her for reasons he'd made clear in the months following their wedding and in the beginning she'd been both flattered that he'd found her desirable and naïve enough to believe that feeling affection for her husband was enough for her to be happily married.

She'd never make that mistake again.

Zoe wasn't exactly sure what she wanted out of her next long-term relationship, but she'd never be with anyone who trifled with her emotions or damaged her self-esteem in any way.

"I am, too," Zoe said. "Tonya was just filling me in on some of the things I could do to help out."

"So you're going to be a regular?"

"I'd like that," Zoe said, glancing Tonya's way to escape his intense scrutiny.

The turmoil raging inside her from her subterfuge, her guilt and her body's chemical reaction to Ryan was a volatile mix. Zoe set her palms together and slid her hands between her thighs to hide their shaking.

"And we're happy to have her," Tonya said, her attention remaining fixed on Ryan.

"Hey, Tonya, could you come here a second?" a man called from across the room.

"Excuse me," she said, getting to her feet. "I'll be right back. Don't go anywhere." This last part she added with a wry smile in Ryan's direction.

With Tonya's departure, Zoe expected Ryan to head off, as well. Instead, he dropped into the chair Tonya had vacated and glanced at the paperwork Zoe had filled out. He glanced up and noticed her watching him. His lopsided smile made her pulse skip.

"I was afraid when you left yesterday that I'd never see you again," he said, the admission making her heart race.

"It just didn't seem like the right time to be here," she murmured, barely able to hear herself over the litany of alerts blaring in her mind.

"Do you want to grab a cup of coffee when you're done here?"

Her initial unguarded reaction was jubilation and she goggled at his invitation like a smitten fool. Ryan was an incredibly sexy man and any woman would be thrilled that he wanted to spend time with her.

But did it make sense that he was interested in her? Not Zoe Crosby the wealthy socialite, but plain Zoe Alston with her spiky hair and inexpensive clothing. In her current state, she recognized she wasn't in his league and he had to know that. So what was his angle and how did she go about finding out without tipping her hand?

Everly had warned her that Ryan was bound to be suspicious if Zoe came on too strong, so she intended to focus all her attention on getting on Susannah's good side. She'd never imagined that Ryan might be interested in her and this odd turn left her tongue-tied while she rethought her strategy.

"Don't look so alarmed," he said, misreading her hesitation. "I'm harmless. Ask anyone here."

"I'm not sure harmless is an accurate description of you," she said.

"No? Then what would you say that I am?"

Charming. Sexy. Irresistible.

Or if Everly was right, he was predatory, manipulative and cruel.

Zoe couldn't picture him like that.

"You seem quite nice."

He laughed. "The way you say that it almost seems like an insult."

"It's not." Her cheeks felt overly warm. "I like nice."

His white teeth flashed in a smile that heated her blood and drew her in until she caught herself leaning into his space. Silver glinted in his gray eyes, mesmerizing her.

"Good," he murmured. "Because I want you to like me."

It unnerved her to discover that she craved his company and that her motivation wasn't due to any revenge plot she'd embroiled herself in. Zoe recognized that her interest in Ryan was purely female and driven by an instinct as old as time. She fingered her short hair and struggled against the pull of his charisma.

"I'm not sure how long they need me to stick around today," she hedged, glancing in Tonya's direction. The woman watched Zoe and Ryan with interest.

"I'll wait." His gray eyes remained fixed on her and their steadiness made Zoe fidget.

"I'm sure you have much better things to do than hang around and wait for me," she said. "Don't you have a company to run?"

He deflected her brush-off with a lazy grin. "One perk of being the boss is that I set my own schedule."

His utter confidence was turning her on. Zoe shifted in her chair. This would not do. There was too much at stake for her to become distracted by an attack of lust.

"Or if you'd prefer," he continued, his deep voice turning her bones—and willpower—to mush. "We could have dinner."

Zoe compelled her gaze to shift away from the determined glint in his eyes, but the damage was done. His unrelenting focus had struck a match to the dry tinder of loneliness she'd endured in her marriage.

"Sure." The word came out in a breathless rush before her thoughts caught up to her emotions. "I mean—"

A broad smile bloomed on his face. "Too late," he said, cutting her off. "Tonight at seven?"

"I'm busy tonight," she lied, remembering that she shouldn't appear too eager.

"Tomorrow?"

"You're awfully determined, aren't you?" She tried to act as if she wasn't flattered by his persistence while a traitorous thrill pulsed deep inside her, setting her nerves to jangling and twisting her stomach into knots.

"I'm used to getting my way."

Indeed. Which was why she'd be wise to keep her wits about her and her defenses on high alert. Her purpose in joining the campaign was to hurt him by causing his sister damage. An eye for an eye, Everly had said.

Zoe hadn't taken into account how difficult it would be to exact revenge on someone she found herself liking. She had to remember that Ryan was a bad guy like her ex-husband. Focusing on that would make it a lot easier to take him down.

Instead she caught herself daydreaming about his handsome face and gorgeous body. But more worrisome than her double-crossing libido was the way his wry humor made her smile and his easy confidence bypassed her defenses. Add in his devotion to his sister and he appeared to be quite the catch.

The question remained. If he was so wonderful, why was he still single? Everly insisted he lacked a conscience. That he had no qualms about using women and then throwing them aside. He'd certainly done that to Kelly Briggs.

And then he'd sent her to jail after she'd acted out, impulsively deleting engineering schematics that had cost his company millions of dollars. Everly wanted him to pay for leading her sister on and then turning his back on her. From the picture Everly had painted of him, Zoe easily perceived him as someone who deserved payback.

But how was she to reconcile that version of Ryan with the man she'd met? The disconnect worried Zoe and made her question the wisdom of what she'd joined Susannah's campaign intending to do.

"Where can I pick you up?" he asked, interrupting her train of thought.

Zoe shook her head. He would expect her to be renting an apartment or a house. Her living arrangements were far less conventional and he would ask too many questions she didn't want to answer.

"How about I meet you at the restaurant?" she suggested.

His eyes narrowed as he surveyed her. "How do I know you'll show up?"

"Why wouldn't I?"

"That's an interesting question." He leaned forward and his powerful presence enveloped her. "There's something about you I can't put my finger on, but you intrigue me."

His declaration gave Zoe goose bumps. And only some of them were the good kind.

"Me?" She huffed out a laugh and shook her head.

"That's funny. There's not a single interesting thing about me."

"Let me be the judge of that. I'm looking forward to getting to know you much better. How about we meet at Charleston Grill at seven?"

The last thing Zoe wanted to do was to eat anywhere close to downtown Charleston where she might run into someone she knew.

"That's a little too fancy for me," she said, thinking fast. "How about Bertha's Kitchen at six?"

The iconic soul food restaurant was located in North Charleston and famous for its fried chicken and Southern sides. The hearty helpings of delicious soul food were served cafeteria-style on no-frills foam plates. Not necessarily a place she'd expect a wealthy businessman like Ryan to dine.

To her surprise, he nodded without hesitation. "I'll see you at six." He pulled a card out of his pocket and handed it to her. "Here's my number if anything changes." When she started to pull it from his fingers, Ryan tightened his grip. "But you have to know I'll be crushed if you stand me up."

She doubted that anything could crush him, but rushed to assure him. "I won't."

With a quick, heart-stopping smile, he got to his feet. "See you tomorrow, Zoe Alston."

"See you tomorrow," she echoed faintly, her whole body buzzing with energy. "Ryan Dailey."

Buzzing with satisfaction, Ryan headed for his sister's office. As he entered, Susannah leaned back in her executive chair and the springs creaked ominously. Although his sister had more than enough money to furnish her campaign office with all new furniture, she'd chosen to downplay her wealth by sticking to a strict budget.

"Thanks for calling me with a heads-up that Zoe had returned," he said, sliding into one of her guest chairs.

"I'm always happy to help out my big brother." Susannah was five minutes younger than Ryan, but her serious nature had always made her seem years older. "Did you ask her out?"

"I invited her to dinner."

Susannah arched an eyebrow. "And is she going?"

"What do you think?" He made no attempt to hide his smirk.

"That she's not exactly your type."

Ryan knew his sister was referring to the fact that all the women he dated came from their social circles. Interchangeable beauties that came from wealth. Good families. Good schools. Good manners. Good careers. By marrying any of them he would've fallen into a predictable pattern. He wanted a woman who riled his emotions and challenged him.

"I'll admit her style isn't what I'm used to, but I'd like to think I'm not that shallow." Ryan flashed a disarming grin. "She's mysterious and there's something tragic in her eyes."

"And deep down inside you have a knight-in-shining-armor complex that gets you into trouble."

Susannah was talking about Kelly Briggs. He'd tried to help her out and the whole thing had backfired.

"Just because you haven't needed my help since middle school doesn't mean others don't appreciate some assistance now and then," he said. "And you're not exactly one to talk. No one likes to help out more than you."

"Help," she said. "Not rescue."

"Zoe doesn't strike me as a woman who needs to be rescued."

"Yet you just said there was something tragic about her. It worries me after what happened with Kelly."

It still bugged Ryan that he'd mishandled the situation with Kelly Briggs. Well, maybe mishandled wasn't the best description for what had happened. He'd taken her at face value and failed to look below the surface for what had motivated her.

From the first Kelly had shown great promise, establishing herself as a clever and talented member of his team. She was also beautiful and if she hadn't been his employee, he might've dated her. They'd had wonderful chemistry both professionally as well as personally. Several times he'd been tempted to cross the line, but he never had.

That wasn't to say things didn't get blurry from time to time. Especially after he'd discovered that Kelly'd had ongoing troubles with an ex-boyfriend who had refused to accept that they were done. Ryan hadn't considered there might be repercussions when he'd come to her rescue one evening in the company parking lot. Or that he might be sending the wrong signals when he'd offered to help her out if the guy came around again.

"What happened with Kelly was a brief lapse in my judgment. And Zoe's different. She's wary and prickly. I think she's been through something difficult and hasn't fully healed."

He had a hard time picturing Zoe as someone who was going to fall for him just because he was nice to her. No, if he wanted Zoe, he was going to have to work damned hard to get her.

"Do you think it's a good idea to get involved with someone like that? Can't you find someone uncomplicated to date?"

"Uncomplicated is boring."

"As an old married woman who adores her husband and two darling children, I can tell you that uncomplicated is perfectly wonderful."

"So much so that you decided to run for office? If you were as completely happy as you claim, then you'd be satisfied with your brilliant law career and perfect home life."

She frowned at him. "That's unfair. Being satisfied doesn't mean you don't want more. Part of being happy with my life is challenging myself and growing as a person. Running for office is part of that."

A knock sounded and Ryan glanced around to see Gil standing in the open doorway. Susannah invited him in and he took the chair beside Ryan.

"What's going on, Gil?" Susannah asked.

"What do you know about the woman you were talking to?" Gil asked Ryan.

"Zoe?" Ryan glanced at his sister to gauge her reaction and saw she was equally puzzled. "I don't know anything about her. Why?"

"I was talking to Tonya and she says she's getting a bad vibe off of her."

"What sort of bad vibe?" Susannah asked, beating Ryan to the punch.

"She's just been very evasive about her background and why she wants to work for the campaign." Gil fixed his gaze on Susannah. "She showed up the day Abernathy announced he was running in this district. I just think the timing is suspicious."

Ryan didn't like what the campaign manager was insinuating. "Suspicious how?"

"What if Lyle sent her here to spy on us."

"Seriously?" Ryan scoffed. "Does she look like a spy?"

"Of course not. That's what makes her so perfect. Tanya said she used a PO Box for her home address and asked a lot of questions about everybody who works here. I think we should do more research on her before giving her anything that would tip our hand about our strategy."

"You have to be kidding about this." Yet even as he continued to argue, Ryan noted a shift in his attitude. His twin's earlier concern that he was intrigued with Zoe reclaimed his attention. Was she another bad choice? Ryan hated that he continued to question his instincts. "Susannah, are you buying this conspiracy theory?"

Another way they were different was in her measured approach to all situations. Where Ryan tended to jump in and deal with the consequences later, Susannah waited, calculating all options before making a move. He liked to think they balanced each other out. She encouraged him to slow down. He persuaded her to follow her gut.

"You're having dinner with her, aren't you?" she asked him. "I agree with Gil that we need to learn a little bit more about her."

To his dismay, Ryan noted an uptick in his own doubts. This campaign meant a great deal to Susannah. She was sacrificing a run at making partner at her law firm and taking time away from her family to chase her political dreams. If something like misplaced trust in a campaign volunteer created problems that led to her losing to a hack like Abernathy, she would be devastated.

"I like this woman," he protested, knowing he would do everything in his power to protect his sister. "I'm not going to treat her like an enemy combatant."

"You don't have to go full-interrogation mode on her," Susannah said with a mocking smile. "Just use that special Ryan Dailey charm of yours and get to know her better." She arched an eyebrow.

"Fine, I will do my duty to the campaign and learn every single detail about her life." He paused, noting that Gil didn't look particularly happy with the exchange. "Why don't you give me a copy of her information form and I'll see what I can find out from Paul?"

Paul Watts, owner of Watts Cyber Security, had helped Ryan figure out who'd sabotaged his engineering firm to the tune of two and a half million dollars and had been instrumental in building a case against Kelly Briggs.

More importantly, he'd been Ryan's best friend

since kindergarten. A fascination with technology had sparked a friendship between the two boys and kept them tight as adults. In addition to growing up in the same neighborhood, they'd attended the same schools through college.

Despite their many similarities, each man had chosen a very different career. Ryan had started his own engineering firm while Paul had turned his back on his family's shipping business, choosing a career in law enforcement instead. That had put him at odds with his father and brother, leading to bitter arguments and an estrangement that went back several years.

Unsure where he might find his friend at the moment, Ryan shot Paul a quick text, suggesting they meet for a drink. Paul was a self-proclaimed workaholic. Often he would get lost in his work and forget to eat and sleep. Things had gotten worse in the last year while he'd chased a gang of cyber thieves who had hacked one of his clients and stolen financial data on tens of thousands of their customers.

I'm home. Stop on by.

Ryan collected Zoe's information form and headed to his car. He looked for her as he strolled through the campaign office, but she was already gone.

After making a couple quick stops, Ryan stood on Paul's front porch armed with cold beer and a loaded pizza from D'Allesandro's. Paul was barefoot and freshly showered when he answered the door, but despite his well-groomed appearance, he had dark circles beneath his forest-green eyes.

"Geez," Ryan commented, shocked at his friend's paleness. "Have you been getting any sleep?"

"I worked all night," Paul muttered as he took the pizza and led the way into his kitchen.

"You do know it's five in the afternoon."

Paul set the box down and raked his fingers through his thick sandy-blond hair. He glanced at the clock on the microwave. "Is it?"

"I don't even want to ask if you're eating." Ryan pushed aside his own issues for the moment so he could focus on his friend. He popped the top on one of the beers and handed it over. "How's Grady doing?"

Grady Watts was Paul's grandfather and one of his biggest influences in life. A man who worked hard and played harder, Grady had been in failing health over the last several years. And things had really gone downhill after he'd suffered a stroke a month ago that affected his speech and paralyzed his right side.

"It's not looking good," Paul replied, his manner grim. He braced his hand on the counter, took a long swig from the bottle and stared off into space. "He just doesn't have the will to get better and I don't know how to reach him."

"Have you talked with your dad and brother about it?"

"What do you think?"

Ryan kept his opinion to himself. He loved his friend, but Paul had a black-and-white view of things that made compromise impossible. And although he'd never admit it, the way his family had refused to support his decision to join the police force had badly hurt him.

"That really sucks," Ryan said. Maybe it was being a twin or the fact that his parents were so supportive of everything he'd done, but Ryan couldn't imagine being estranged from any of his immediate family. "Is there anything I can do to help?"

A ghost of a smile crossed Paul's lips. "You're here with pizza and beer."

Ryan winced. "Well, it's not exactly an altruistic visit." He pulled out the copy of Zoe's information form and slid it along the marble-topped kitchen island toward his friend. "I have someone I need you to check out."

"Who is she?"

"Someone who recently joined Susannah's campaign and Gil is suspicious of her. He thinks she might be a spy for Lyle Abernathy."

"Why would that matter?"

"Have you come up for air at all in the last few days?" Ryan asked, his tone split between amusement and frustration. "Abernathy has switched districts and entered the state senate race against Susannah."

"I guess I heard something about it but didn't put two and two together." Paul grabbed a slice of pizza and took a bite while perusing the sheet of paper with Zoe's information. "So what do you think is going on with Zoe Alston?"

"I'm reserving judgment."

For a long moment Paul studied his friend. "Are you attracted to her?"

"Yes."

"So is this really about your sister's campaign or are you having me investigate her because of what happened with Kelly Briggs?"

"Maybe a little of both," Ryan admitted, hating that he no longer trusted his gut when it came to women he was drawn to. "Look, there's nothing wrong with erring on the side of caution. And I'm not the one who raised the alarm."

While that was true, it was also the case that he wasn't rushing to defend Zoe as innocent. Gil's paranoia had aroused Ryan's suspicions and they weren't going away without concrete proof that she wasn't a threat to Susannah.

"I'll check into her," Paul said. "Just promise me you'll back off if I turn up anything."

Ryan recalled the hit to his libido dealt by Zoe's delectable scent, lean curves and full lips. Something about her put his senses on full alert and he doubted he'd be able to walk away without getting her into bed first.

"I'll think about it," he said, knowing he would do no such thing.

Three

Zoe was fretting about the dinner date she'd made with Ryan Dailey the previous day as she walked through the front door of Second Chance Treasures. She'd opened the boutique featuring arts and crafts items made by women who'd been victims of domestic violence a year ago. The concept for the project had been inspired by the helplessness Zoe had felt while married to Tristan. Usually, the store imbued her with an uplifting sense of pride and accomplishment, but more and more lately she'd been weighed down by looming dread as her bank balance dwindled.

From fledgling idea to breaking even, the project had been Zoe's passion for three years. In that time she'd been able to help nearly a hundred women who struggled financially after fleeing their troubled marriages.

With each month that passed, both her inventory and her customer base grew. Unfortunately, in getting to this point, she'd put everything she had into the store only to find it wasn't enough.

She was behind on her rent and on the verge of failing everyone who so desperately needed her to pull off a win. The ever-increasing financial pressure was part of what had goaded her into entering the revenge plot with Everly and London. The possibility that London might find a clue that would point Zoe in the direction of the money Tristan had hidden offshore combined with longing to see her ex-husband suffer for the pain he'd put her through was what had drawn Zoe into Everly's scheme.

"Hey, Jessica," she called to her part-time helper standing behind the counter. "How'd we do today?"

"Something horrible happened," the twenty-five-year-old mother of two wailed, heartbreak in her voice. "And it's all my fault."

Zoe rushed to her, tamping down panic. The last thing she needed to do was to overreact. "I'm sure it's not your fault," she said, coming close enough to see that Jessica's blue eyes were rimmed in red. She'd obviously been crying. "What happened? Are you okay? No one hurt you, did they?"

"No." Jessica shook her head vehemently. "Nothing like that. All the cash that was supposed to go to the bank today is gone."

Zoe bit back a moan as she absorbed the financial hit and wrapped her arms around the distraught woman. "It's okay. Why don't you tell me what happened?"

"I wanted to catch Ashley's program at school so

Maggie came in just before lunch to watch the store for me," Jessica began, her breath shuddering as tears began to fall.

Although Maggie had limited artistic or crafts experience, she'd helped out at the store whenever possible. Zoe had always found her reliable and trustworthy. "You think she took the money?"

Jessica's shoulders rose and fell. She looked miserable. "When I came back she bolted out of here and I thought it was really strange. It didn't occur to me until an hour later that I hadn't locked the cash into the bank deposit bag before I left. When I went into the back to check on it, the money was gone."

"It's okay," Zoe repeated even though that was the furthest thing from the truth.

Dozens of women were counting on her to pay them for the inventory they'd put their hearts and souls into and she'd promised the landlord she'd catch up on several months' worth of past-due lease payments. Zoe guessed there had been nearly five thousand dollars in cash ready to be deposited. This was all her fault. She'd been distracted by her work with Susannah's campaign and had neglected to get to the bank for nearly a week.

"How was Maggie acting when she came in today?"

"I don't know." Jessica scrunched up her face as she thought. "Maybe a little distracted. She's been that way a lot lately. I think something might be going on with her ex."

"Has she talked to you about him?"

Even as she asked the question, Zoe knew the likely answer was no. Domestic violence was a silent epidemic with many victims either too afraid or too ashamed to speak out against their abuser.

"No," Jessica said, confirming what Zoe had assumed to be the case. "You know how Maggie is."

Magnolia Fenton had three children and an ex-husband with a hair-trigger temper. While he'd never been physically abusive, his systematic belittling and shaming of Maggie, and the way he'd cut her off from family and friends, had taken its toll.

Add to that her lack of marketable skills that kept her from getting a job and saving money and Maggie had felt completely trapped. Her situation resonated with Zoe because of her own experiences and she'd tried sharing her story in an attempt to connect with Maggie. Over the last few months Zoe had believed she was making progress. And now this.

"I'm sure Maggie had a good reason for taking the money," Zoe said, hoping that was true. "She isn't a thief." Something dire would have to be happening for her to do something so drastic.

"Are you going to call the police?" Jessica wrung her hands. She already blamed herself for what had happened and if Zoe reached out to the authorities, no doubt the other woman would never forgive herself.

"No." That was the last thing Maggie needed. "I'll give her a call and hopefully we can figure out what's going on."

Zoe wasn't surprised when her attempt to reach Maggie ended in the phone being out of service. From their conversations, Zoe had learned that Maggie's ex had stalked her after she'd left and even gone so far as to damage her car. The way he'd isolated Maggie had triggered powerful emotions in Zoe and she recognized she'd retreated from Maggie when she should've stepped up and become her champion.

At three o'clock Jessica headed off to meet her children's school bus, leaving Zoe by herself. Fortunately a steady stream of customers entering the store kept Zoe from dwelling on her problems. But as five rolled around and she locked the front door, anxiety-raising thoughts swarmed her tired brain.

The business card Ryan had given her was on her desk in the back room. Given what was going on with her store, Zoe could've justified canceling that night's dinner with Ryan. But the man was a whole lot of distracting and, whether she liked it or not, the way he made her feel was exciting.

Zoe ruthlessly pushed aside her reaction to the man's charm and reminded herself that her real purpose in going out with him was to glean as much information as she could about his sister and her campaign. Bypassing an elegant sheath in her favorite shade of blue, Zoe chose a black-and-white-striped T-shirt dress, white sneakers and an oversize black cardigan. The outfit was similar to something she would've worn in her college days. Comfortable and down to earth, without a designer label in sight. Not exactly guaranteed to stop a man in his tracks.

Making herself forgettable was important if she was to get the goods on Susannah's campaign without calling attention to herself. If Ryan continued to pursue her, Zoe would be a topic of conversation among the staff.

Yesterday, after Ryan had gone in to talk to his sister, Tonya had made it pretty clear that Zoe should maintain her distance from the candidate's twin brother. Tonya's reasoning had been a little muddy, but her irritation had come through crystal clear.

Zoe had made a point of declaring she wasn't interested in Ryan, but Tonya had obviously not believed her. The subtext being that no woman in her right mind could resist him. That question was front and center in Zoe's thoughts as she parked her car and spied Ryan waiting for her near the front door.

As she walked toward him, she gave herself several seconds to admire his lean, muscular form clad in worn jeans and a long-sleeved, black knit shirt with the cuffs pushed up to reveal his strong forearms. He appeared completely at ease in the modest surroundings.

Bertha's Kitchen was housed in a two-story building painted robin's-egg blue and trimmed in purple. Founded in 1979, the restaurant was a primer in Lowcountry soul food and one of Zoe's favorite places to stop whenever she made a trip to North Charleston to volunteer at the animal shelter.

"Hi," she said as she stepped within earshot. "Sorry I'm late. The traffic was worse than I expected."

"Not to worry," he said with a smoky half smile. "You are worth waiting for."

At a loss for a clever response, Zoe regarded him in silence. She was accustomed to a certain amount of flattery. Tristan's friends had often commented on her beauty, but those remarks had always seemed to be for her husband's benefit, speaking to Tristan's potency that other men found his wife desirable.

Yet here she stood in her ordinary clothes and Ryan behaved as if she was the most well-dressed woman on the planet. Electricity sparked along her nerve endings, making her hyperaware that his skin radiated the wholesome scent of soap and his shampoo made her think of sunshine.

"Are you hungry?" she asked, grasping at the first safe subject that popped into her mind in an effort to keep the conversation rolling. "The food here is fantastic. Although probably not the sort of fare you're used to."

"On the contrary, I come here fairly often." He gestured for her to precede him into the restaurant. "More so now that Susannah's campaign headquarters is nearby."

Her lame attempt to point out their social differences and demonstrate that she wasn't the sort of highbrow date he was used to had failed miserably. Zoe reassessed her impression of Ryan as he grinned and flirted with the women dishing out plates of fried pork chops, fried chicken, stewed greens, dark roux okra soup and moist cornbread. It was pretty obvious he hadn't been exaggerating about being a regular because he knew several of the servers and kitchen staff by name and they all knew him.

By the time they carried their trays of food and sweet tea to a table, Zoe was feeling utterly defeated.

"Tell me about yourself," Ryan said, skipping small

talk and jumping straight in. "I want to know everything."

She'd expected that he'd be like most successful men of her acquaintance and only interested in talking about himself. While she'd prepared a dull story that would ensure he'd lose interest quickly, something about his direct gaze warned her she'd better watch what she said.

"I'm pretty ordinary," she began, selling her claim with a lackluster tone and cultivated casualness. The struggle to maintain her blasé façade while her pulse hammered away highlighted Ryan's powerful effect on her. "You're the one who's interesting. You run a successful engineering firm with projects all over the world."

Unfortunately, Ryan wasn't distracted by her attempt to deflect the attention away from herself. "Where did you grow up?"

"Greenville."

If Ryan was determined to mine her background, Zoe intended to keep her answers short and vague.

"What brought you to Charleston?"

"I came here after college."

She left out the part about being a brand-new bride bubbling with optimism about her new life with her handsome, wealthy husband. In the early days of her marriage she'd thought her life was going to be perfect.

"Where did you go to school?"

"University of South Carolina."

"Major?"

"I never graduated."

He cocked his head at her defensive tone. "You say that like you expect me to judge you."

"You're a brilliant engineer and a successful businessman," she said. "Your sister is a lawyer who's running for state senate." *I'm not in your league.*

"And because you didn't graduate college that somehow makes you less worthy?" He paused a beat before adding, "Or are you just passing judgment on me by assuming I think I'm better than everyone else? Is that why you wanted to come here? To point out that you're one of the people while I'm an entitled jerk?"

"No." But wasn't that exactly why she'd chosen Bertha's Kitchen?

"Then why make such a big deal about me being successful?" He asked like he was curious about her motivation. As if he was interested in getting to know her. Like he intended to uncover all her secrets. Her breath hitched at the danger this presented.

"I guess I've become accustomed to being judged for my choices."

"Are you happy with the decisions you made?"

"Is anyone?" The items in her poor judgment column definitely outweighed the accomplishments she was proud of.

"What would you go back and change if you could?"

Over the last few years Zoe had given the matter a great deal of thought. Her marriage to Tristan hadn't been all bad. He could be kind and funny and generous. At least, early on that had been the case. She'd been a naïve twenty when they'd gotten married and easy for him to control. She'd wanted to please Tristan and most of the time she had.

"That's a tough question to answer. The decisions I made helped me to become who I am today. I like that person. Other choices might have resulted in me becoming someone else."

"Do you wish you'd graduated?"

"Of course I wish I'd graduated." Yet was that completely true? She'd disliked the major she'd chosen and had struggled through her classes. When Tristan had insisted he couldn't wait to make her his wife, she'd happily forgone her senior year. It wasn't until she'd moved to Charleston that she'd realized her mistake.

The social circle Tristan moved in had been filled with beautiful former debutantes—with college degrees—who'd loved to talk about their alma maters. Zoe had always felt a little foolish for not completing her education.

"What did you major in?"

"Hospitality management." She made a face. "I went to college because everyone expected me to." At eighteen she'd been unable to visualize her future without that step. Unable or unwilling? Her family had expected her to go. Had she even considered what would be best for her? "I really didn't have a sense of what I wanted to do."

"Looking back, what do you wish you'd done instead?"

"Sociology or counseling." For a while she'd considered going back to school, but Tristan hadn't seen the purpose, pointing out that she didn't need a degree to be Mrs. Tristan Crosby. "I'd like to be able to help people."

"I'll bet you'd be good at it."

She wanted to point out that he didn't know her well enough to make that assessment, but the compelling light in his gray eyes left her wondering if maybe he saw deeper inside her than she realized. The thought unnerved her. And yet she was also flattered that he was making the effort to look beneath her surface.

No doubt about it. Ryan Dailey was a complicated guy who aroused complex emotions in her. That made him more dangerous than she might be able to handle.

"Can we talk about something else?" she asked. "I'm really not all that interesting."

"You don't give yourself enough credit," he teased, despite the somber feeling stealing over him.

His initial assessment that Zoe's edgy exterior protected a delicate core was proving true. Her insistence that there wasn't much he might find interesting about her intrigued him. Instead of convincing him she was ordinary, he grew even more curious about what she was hiding. And why.

"One last question," he insisted, ignoring her weary exhalation. "What do you do when you're not volunteering for my sister's campaign?"

"I work at a boutique store in downtown Charleston. Second Chance Treasures."

Her quick answer surprised him. As did the way her spine straightened and her chin came up. Her whole manner brightened. She stopped avoiding his gaze and made eye contact. The beauty of her light brown eyes hit him full-force. For long seconds he lost his train of thought but finally shook himself free of her spell.

"What do you sell there?"

"We specialize in arts and crafts items made by women who are survivors of domestic abuse. Every sale helps them on their road to financial independence." There was pride in Zoe's voice.

From the beginning he'd thought her beautiful, but now, as she spoke about the store, her bright smile and fierce satisfaction captivated him. "Sounds less like a job and more like a calling for you."

As if realizing she might have given too much away, she dialed back her emotions. With a careless shrug, she murmured, "It feels good to help out."

He agreed but sensed she wouldn't accept any overture he might make. She obviously wasn't ready to trust him, but would she accept aid from a different quarter?

"It sounds like something my sister would be interested in helping with," he said. "Have you mentioned the store to her?"

Zoe shook her head. "She's busy with the campaign. I wouldn't want to bother her."

"You wouldn't be bothering her," he insisted, recognizing that the issue of domestic violence was something his sister could take up in her campaign. "In fact, having an event at your store might be good PR for both of you. It might be worth asking the owner about."

"I suppose I could do that."

Her vague answer left Ryan wondering if she actually would. Regardless, he decided to suggest Susannah check out the store. Even if an event couldn't be organized, Ryan knew his twin would do what she could to help out.

"You seem like the perfect person to be on Susannah's team," Ryan said, turning his attention to the onerous task of deciding if Zoe was in any way connected to Abernathy's campaign. "You have the sort of passion to effect social change that drew my sister to public office. Have you volunteered for any other campaigns?"

"No."

Zoe's short answer left Ryan regretting that he'd been too direct in his inquiry. Why not just come out and ask her if she was spying for Abernathy?

"Why now then?"

She became absorbed in pushing her uneaten lima beans into a neat line on her plate.

"I guess I realized that nothing is going to change unless people get involved."

"People?" he asked, nudging her to clarify.

A dry smile quickly passed across her lovely lips. "Unless I get involved."

"I think a lot of people are feeling that way," Ryan agreed. "Susannah said their volunteer list has doubled since Abernathy announced he was running."

"That isn't surprising. He's a terrible politician."

"You sound familiar with him."

She shook her head. "Not at all. It's just what I've heard."

While her denial didn't ring true, it was pretty obvious that her disgust was genuine. Maybe a little too obvious? Demonstrating an unfavorable opinion about

Lyle Abernathy didn't exactly clear her of being a spy. Clearly she couldn't come right out and sing the guy's praises while volunteering for Susannah's campaign.

Ryan wished his gut wasn't warning him that her explanation for joining his sister's campaign wasn't the whole story. Clearing Zoe of suspicion would've opened the path to pursing her romantically. That Gil and his sister could be right to suspect her churned in Ryan's stomach like acid. He'd hoped she'd ease his mind over dinner. Instead she'd awakened more questions.

Obviously he would have to continue investigating her.

"Thank you for dinner," she said as they exited the restaurant and headed for the parking lot.

"You're welcome," Ryan said, matching her slow pace. "Maybe next time you'll let me pick the place."

Zoe reached her car and turned to face Ryan. Every line of her body, her tense muscles and slight frown, screamed reluctance.

"Look," she began, obviously gearing up to blow him off. "You are a really nice guy, but this isn't going to work."

Ryan set his hands on his hips and wondered if she was as immune to him as she appeared. "Because?"

"We're way too different." She waved her hand between them as if to demonstrate her point.

"Being different is what makes things interesting," he countered, taking a step in her direction.

Her eyes widened as he invaded her space. "Being different is what leads to problems. You like champagne. I like beer."

"You like beer?" he echoed in surprise, unsure why he couldn't picture her with a bottle in her hand.

"Well, no," she admitted. "I usually drink vodka, but you get what I'm saying. You're South of Broad and I'm…" She trailed off as if her current address eluded her.

"Where do you live?"

"I'm crashing with a friend at the moment," she said, her whole manner evasive. "See, that's what I mean. You're rich and I can't afford to rent an apartment. It would never work."

"I disagree and frankly I'm a little insulted that you're judging me on my financial situation."

"You're insulted?" She crossed her arms over her chest and stuck her chin out.

"Yes. And I think you're lying about why you don't want to see me again."

"I'm not."

He ignored her denial and plowed on. "I think you're proud of your self-reliance to the point where you refuse to accept anyone's help no matter how dire your situation." From the way her eyes widened, Ryan saw that his point had struck home. "What are you afraid of?"

"I'm not afraid," she countered. "But you're right about my pride. It's important to me that I do it on my own."

Her fierceness fired his desire and forced him to shove his hands into his pockets to stop from snatching her into his arms and setting his lips to hers. Skittish and assertive in turns, she was a complex knot for him to unravel. The question remained whether or not he should.

"One more date," he declared. "We'll have dinner this weekend. Any place you want."

She shook her head. "You aren't going to take no for an answer, are you?"

"I like you. A lot. I think you like me, too." He paused, offering her the opportunity to disagree. When she didn't jump in, he had his answer. "Good. Saturday night at six. I'll be in touch to finalize the details."

"You're wasting your time," she declared, but her voice lacked conviction. "Good night, Ryan Dailey."

"Sweet dreams, Zoe Alston."

As she slid behind the wheel of her gray Subaru, Ryan headed to his own vehicle. He remained bothered that she'd listed a PO Box number as her home address and claimed to be staying with a friend. Why so vague about where she lived? What secrets was she trying to keep hidden?

Ryan was determined to find out and as she exited the parking lot, he let her get a little ahead of him before slipping into traffic behind her. He doubted his sister would approve of him tailing Zoe, but he wouldn't be able to rest unless he was satisfied that Zoe was telling the truth about her living situation.

From where they'd had dinner, it was a straight shot to downtown Charleston. As he tailed Zoe, Ryan wondered if he'd have done something like this before his troubles with Kelly Briggs. He'd never considered himself naïve when it came to women, but after the way he'd misread Kelly, Ryan's first impulse was to assume the worst. He wasn't proud of his newly cynical perspective or the way it warred with his innate desire to give people the benefit of the doubt. Being suspicious tainted him somehow.

When Highway 52 became King Street and Zoe's car continued straight on, Ryan suspected she wasn't heading home but rather to one of the downtown bars. This was where things could get dicey. He'd have to follow her in to see what she was up to, all the while staying out of sight.

But even as Ryan pondered how to accomplish this, Zoe turned onto a side street and parked behind a retail building. Ryan kept going, but slowed to read the name painted on the windows of the darkened store. Second Chance Treasures. The place where Zoe said she worked. What could she possibly be doing there so late?

Ryan circled the block and found a place down the street where he could observe the parking lot and keep track of who showed up. After an hour, all remained quiet and Ryan's curiosity morphed into frustration. The entire back of the building was windowless, offering no clue as to what could be going on inside. Additionally, Zoe's car was the only one in the parking lot. Unless someone had arrived on foot before he'd showed up, Ryan had to assume she was alone.

Frustrated by the lack of action, he put his car back in gear and cruised past the front again. Tapping his fingers on the steering wheel, he headed for his nineteenth-century Queen Anne house north of downtown.

He'd bought the home a couple of years ago after a major renovation had resulted in the replacement of the antiquated plumbing and electrical. Sitting on half an acre, the seven-thousand-square-foot home was way more space than he needed, but he loved the yard and the pair of one-bedroom apartments at the back of the property the previous owners had rented out. Ryan didn't need the hassle of tenants or the extra income, but he appreciated having additional space, separate from the main house, where he could put up out-of-town guests.

After parking in the three-car garage, Ryan made his way across the backyard and into his all-white, ultra-modern kitchen. Most people looking for a historical house would've been annoyed that the home's original character hadn't been maintained inside. Ryan appreciated the marble countertops, professional appliances and updated fixtures. The single nod to the home's age was the fireplace along one wall, painted white to blend in. For the rest of the home's styling, Ryan had chosen white for the walls to play up the original pine flooring and selected furniture pieces with clean lines and neutral tones and paired them with large abstract art pieces.

When visiting for the first time, people were struck by the contrast between the historic exterior and modern minimalist interior. Not everyone approved, but Ryan hadn't gotten to where he was by being swayed by other people's opinions.

He poured himself a drink and collapsed onto the couch in his living room with the TV remote in one hand and a crystal tumbler of bourbon in the other. He surfed the local news and stopped when he saw photos of his sister and Lyle Abernathy.

How long would it take for Abernathy to start stirring up trouble? His constituents had grown sick of his antics and he'd been facing a primary challenge in his home district that he was almost sure to lose. That's why he'd switched to Susannah's district. That he'd brought his dirty politics with him made Ryan grind his teeth.

He shut off the TV just as his cell rang.

"Nothing much came up during my initial search on Zoe Alston," Paul began, wasting little time on preliminaries.

"What does that mean?" Ryan asked, his suspicion intensifying at an equal pace with his disappointment. He'd counted on Zoe being as ordinary as she claimed.

"That she doesn't have any current social media presence or obvious electronic trail."

"So, she doesn't exist? Does that mean she gave us a false name?"

"Not false," Paul corrected. "She's recently divorced and back to using her maiden name."

"How recent?"

"A few days. The ink has barely had time to dry."

A powerful wave of relief blindsided Ryan, making him slightly light-headed. Her skittish behavior made a lot more sense. As did the reason why she'd been so reluctant to go out with him. She wasn't a spy, but someone who'd suffered a heartbreak. No doubt she wasn't ready to bare her soul to a stranger.

"Whom was she married to?" Ryan asked.

"Tristan Crosby."

"Sounds familiar." The name rang a faint bell, but Ryan couldn't recall where he'd heard it before.

"He runs Crosby Automotive. The family also owns Crosby Motorsports. The racing team."

A lightbulb went off in Ryan's mind. "Harrison Crosby drives for them."

"That's his younger brother."

So, Zoe's past was a lot more interesting than she'd admitted. And all her excuses about them being from vastly different worlds were a load of crap. Why not just explain that she wasn't ready to date and leave it at that? Why the fabrication?

The questions renewed Ryan's distrust.

"Can you do a background check on the owner of a store? Second Chance Treasures." Ryan gave Paul the address. "And maybe the person who owns the building, as well."

"Can I assume this is tied into your interest in Zoe Alston?"

"Yes. I can't explain why, but there's something up with her and I intend to get to the bottom of it."

"I'll see what I can find out." Paul paused a beat before adding, "You know not every woman has bad intentions."

Not every woman. But he wasn't about to drop his guards again unless he was sure he wouldn't get burned. If being overly suspicious kept his business, family and friends safe, then that's just the way it had to be.

"I…feel something for this one," he said, the confession coming from out of nowhere. "I just want to make sure she checks out."

"I get it." Paul's sober response mirrored Ryan's

mood. "Give me a couple days to see what I can find out."

Stung by impatience, Ryan got to his feet. To hell with waiting a couple days for answers. No reason he couldn't do a little investigating of his own. He grabbed his keys and headed for his car. Too many questions swirled through his brain about Zoe Alston. There was no way he was getting any rest until he'd confronted her with what she'd not told him tonight.

Ryan noticed the uptick in his mood as he slid behind the wheel and recognized its origins. He was eager to see her again. Cursing, Ryan wondered if his sister had been right to warn him off. Obviously Zoe Alston was trouble. Perhaps not for Susannah's campaign, but definitely for his peace of mind.

Four

In the wake of her dinner with Ryan, Zoe had a hard time concentrating on the spreadsheet she'd created to chart her cash flow. Today's disastrous theft by Magnolia Fenton meant she had to figure out which bills she paid and which ones got pushed back a few weeks to a month. At the top of her priority list were the commission payments to the women who provided her inventory. They were counting on those dollars to feed and house their children.

Zoe rubbed her dry eyes and swallowed the bile that rose in her throat. She hated the wave of hopelessness that washed over her. Where could she possibly get more money? The obvious answer came from Ryan's suggestion that she talk to his sister. He was right that an event at the store would both benefit Susannah and bring awareness to Second Chance Treasures. She wished she knew how to overcome her reluctance to ask for help. Sure, she'd been burned in the past when she'd reached out, but Susannah wasn't at all like the women in her former social circle. She couldn't see Ryan's sister being nice to her face while stabbing her in the back.

When she picked up the cup of peppermint tea beside her laptop, Zoe noticed the black smudge of eye makeup on her hand and headed into the bathroom to wash her face. As she patted her skin dry, she scanned her features in the mirror, deciding without the dark makeup she looked younger than her twenty-nine years. At least until she met her reflected gaze and saw the weight of her experiences lingering in her eyes.

A knock sounded on the door that led from the stockroom to the parking lot, making Zoe's heart jump. A glance at her watch showed it was nearly ten at night. Who could possibly be stopping by at this late hour?

Many of the women she worked with knew Zoe's story and that she was living in the store's back room to save money. Opening up about her troubles hadn't been easy for Zoe. She'd spent nearly the whole of her marriage acting as if her life was perfect. But being authentic with these women was important for them and for her. As a result, Zoe was learning courage where she'd once feared. What she'd perceived as weakness and failure didn't have to define her.

With these thoughts lightening her steps, Zoe crossed to the door and opened it. The person standing outside wasn't at all whom she expected.

"What are you doing here?" Zoe asked, hoping her panic didn't show.

"I thought we should talk."

His gaze slid over her, rousing Zoe to the realization that her flowered loungewear and pink fuzzy slippers weren't in keeping with her badass chick persona.

"So you just show up here?" she demanded, outrage lending her the strength to stand her ground and glare at him when her instincts urged her to retreat. "And how did you know where to find me?"

"I followed you."

"You followed...?"

An overwhelming sense of anxiety pummeled her. Yet, even as she backed up a step and started to pull the door closed, she recognized that with his suspicions aroused, this man wouldn't trust her unless she gave him a chance to vent his doubts. Squashing her anxiety, she fell back and let him pass.

Ryan entered the back room, glancing around as he did so. Boxes filled with inventory occupied nearly a third of the wide room. A curtain divided the rest of the space into a staff break room and Zoe's office and living quarters. During the hours when the store was open, Zoe kept the curtain closed, but when she was alone, she tied it back. At the moment the cot she was sleeping on was visible.

"Are you sleeping here?" he asked, his hard gaze returning to her.

Shame sifted through her at her current circumstances. More than anything she'd like to be living like a normal person in a home with a proper kitchen and bathroom.

Instead of answering, she crossed her arms over her chest. "I have work to do. If you would quickly say whatever is on your mind, I can get back to it."

"Fine," he snapped, frowning. "Why didn't you tell me who you were?"

"I told you I'm—"

"Zoe Alston." He nodded. "What you didn't say is that you were formerly Zoe Crosby."

Zoe froze as horror filled her. He'd investigated her. The implications ricocheted through her mind, moving too fast for her to settle on any single reason to freak out. Did he know what she, Everly and London had been up to? Could he be there to threaten her? He hadn't hesitated to send Kelly Briggs to jail. What would he do to Zoe if he knew she'd intended to cause trouble for his sister?

"So I was married," she murmured, hating how exposed she felt at the moment. "It didn't work out." It got a little easier each time she admitted the failure. There was power in that. "What's the big deal?"

"The big deal is that you were acting odd."

"I wasn't." Or at least she'd been trying not to. The man made her nervous with his sharp mind and flagrant sex appeal.

"And you lied."

Lies of omission and of intent. Even so, she refused to apologize or to defend herself. Instead she let her stony expression speak for her.

When the silence stretched, Ryan continued. "You told Tonya you were crashing with a friend."

"Given everything that's happened to me in the last year, forgive me if I didn't feel much like bringing up all my dirty laundry."

"Did you really think anyone would care about your divorce?"

"In my experience, people are quick to judge. All I wanted to do was to help out someone I admired. Now you have to go and ruin that."

Bold words. She might have to follow through and quit the campaign to demonstrate her proclaimed level of outrage wasn't false. How was she supposed to mess up Susannah's campaign if that happened? Of course, there was always the possibility that Lyle Abernathy would succeed where Zoe failed and she could ride off into the sunset without the campaign's blood on her hands.

"Is that why you invited me to dinner?" she asked, feeling deflated. "So you could check me out?"

"No, I invited you out because I was attracted to you."

Pleasure short-circuited the steady rhythm of her breath. But she wondered if he still felt the same now that he'd seen her stripped of her makeup and the tough-girl clothes.

"I'm not your type," she said, returning to the same argument she'd used in the restaurant parking lot.

"How can you be so sure?" he asked, his eyes narrowing as he studied her.

"We might never have crossed paths at any of

Charleston's social functions," she said, on safer ground now that they were talking about him, "but I've seen you out and about. Not to mention all the gossip surrounding the romantic intrigues of one of the city's most eligible bachelors." She gave him a cool smile. "I seem to recall you tend to favor leggy brunettes with blue eyes."

She had no idea if that was true, but enjoyed a stab of satisfaction when his brow wrinkled in surprise.

"I don't know if that's fully accurate." But obviously it was accurate enough.

To emphasize her point, Zoe ran her fingers through her short, spiky hair in a mocking salute. "I am neither brunette nor leggy. And my eyes are not blue."

"No, they are not. They remind me of autumn leaves."

To her dismay, he took a leisurely step in her direction, lowered his lashes and looked her over with predatory intent. Her pulse kicked into high gear when his gaze lingered on her lips and she had a hard time resisting the urge to nibble the lower one. The air in the room seemed suddenly supercharged with erotic energy and Zoe's nipples tightened in anticipation.

"I'm not interested in getting involved with you," she said, throwing up a warning hand even as she sensed that nothing she could do or say would stop the inevitability of their sexual chemistry.

"Then why did you agree to have dinner with me?"

Losing the battle against his magnetism, she replied, "My budget for dining out is extremely tight."

"Is that why you're living here?" Without taking his

eyes from her, Ryan gestured with his head, indicating her cot.

She was abruptly bombarded by an image of them together on the narrow bed, his mouth on hers, his hands diving beneath her clothes, setting fire to her skin. As her blood pounded in her ears, she almost didn't hear Ryan's next question.

"Because you're out of money?"

"Not that it's any of your business," she began, irritated with herself for letting him get to her. "But between my extensive and contentious divorce and opening the boutique, I'm broke."

"You said you worked here," he reminded her. "But you actually own it?"

She nodded.

"That's why you spoke so passionately about the store during dinner."

She nodded again. "I've poured everything into Second Chance Treasures and we're starting to show a small profit, but not quite enough yet."

One dark eyebrow went up, but something akin to approval flickered in his gray eyes as he asked his next question.

"How long have you been living here?"

"Nearly six months. As my divorce dragged on, I gave up my apartment so I could pay the lease here." Zoe had no idea why she was pouring out her problems to Ryan, but it offered her some relief to share her troubles with someone.

"Are you waiting on a settlement?"

Zoe shook her head. "I barely received enough to pay my lawyer."

"Because you signed a prenuptial agreement?"

"That and according to Tristan's financial records, he's heavily mortgaged on every piece of property he owns. He maintains a lavish lifestyle." Her voice grew bitter. "Keeping his prize stable of polo ponies happy and healthy is very expensive."

"But—"

Zoe broke in. "Believe me, I hired the best lawyer I could afford and we looked at everything."

At least everything they knew to look at. Based on Tristan's spending, he had to have been hiding money somewhere. Yet tracing it had proved impossible.

Zoe's thoughts went back in time to that Beautiful Women Taking Charge event and the investigation London was doing on Zoe's behalf. A tiny portion of her held out hope that the event planner might just find something that Zoe could use to take Tristan back to court.

"Looks like you have a fair amount of money tied up in inventory." Ryan indicated the stacks of boxes before striding toward the door that led to the main part of the store.

"I mostly operate on a consignment basis." She trailed after Ryan, letting her fingers drift over the wall until they encountered the light switches. She flipped them on and the space was bathed in a soothing glow. "I buy outright from some of my artists because I want exclusive rights to their work, but most of what I sell I take a fifteen percent commission."

"Wouldn't you be better off owning the inventory?" he asked.

"Probably." Zoe straightened a rack of children's dresses made from organic cotton and nontoxic dyes. "But at first I couldn't afford to buy everything and the women make more by going the consignment route. Now, have I answered all your questions?"

"All but one."

"Fire away."

"Did you join Susannah's campaign on behalf of anyone connected to Lyle Abernathy?"

"What?" Surprise and relief flashed through her in rapid succession. "No. Of course not. Why would I work for Lyle Abernathy?" she asked, the truth coming easily. "I don't know the man. Or anyone connected to him."

Doubt was written all over Ryan's face.

"Look, I can see you don't believe me," she said. "And I will admit that I wasn't up front with you about my past. But if I'm guilty of concealing anything, it's who I am. Ending my marriage to Tristan caused a complete severing of every social tie I had. To the women I used to call friends, I am a pariah. Not one of them has reached out to me since I separated from Tristan."

Hurt gave her voice a quaver. She didn't try to control it. Appearing vulnerable would deflect Ryan's suspicions. Still, discovering that this bothered her surprised Zoe. Those women had never truly been her friends and she should be happy that she was free of their petty mischief.

"I was looking for a fresh start with people who wouldn't judge me based on a preconceived notion of who I was. So I changed my hair and bought some new clothes and joined your sister's campaign because I believe she's going to make a great state senator."

Through her tirade, Ryan remained silent, his expression unreadable.

"I won't apologize for following you here or checking you out," Ryan said. "This senate race is really important to my sister and I won't let anyone mess it up for her. So, if certain events have happened in the past year to make me suspicious as hell of people—"

"People?" she countered, interrupting him. "Or women?"

A muscle twitched in his cheek. "Look, I got burned because I didn't see certain signs," he admitted. But his candidness lasted no longer than a camera flash. "And I'll be damned if I let anything like that happen again."

"I can tell you exactly how to avoid any trouble with me." At his disgruntled snort, she set one hand on her hip and gestured with the other toward the back of the store. "You can walk right out of here and never bother me again."

After leaving Zoe, Ryan had headed home and spent several hours searching the internet for anything he could find on Zoe Crosby. There'd been less than he expected, but the few photos he'd found showed a slender woman with long, straight hair the color of caramel and a Mona Lisa smile. Tranquil and immediately forgettable, despite her beauty, she looked nothing like the spitfire standing before him in pastel floral pajamas and fuzzy slippers.

It struck him then that he didn't want to avoid the trouble she was likely to bring into his life. He wanted to wade right into danger and say to hell with consequences just so he could go on feeling the fierce emotions raging in him. He didn't trust her. He was convinced that much of what she'd told him tonight was grounded in truth, but not the entire story.

That his instincts continued to howl at him warned Ryan he should do as she suggested and never see her again. But his blood pulsed hot and fast through his veins, setting his entire body on fire. From their first encounter, he'd wanted her. Now that he had a better sense of who she was, the craving to slide his fingers over her naked skin was nearly painful in its intensity.

Ryan ground his teeth while his mind fought his body for control. Indulging his desire for her would be madness. Even if she hadn't joined the campaign as one of Abernathy's puppets, it was obvious that whatever she'd been through in the last year—maybe even her entire marriage—had left wounds that were far from healed.

He should just walk away. And in fact, he took several steps, intending to leave the store and never look back. But when he drew even with her, her tantalizing perfume tickled his nose, reminding him of the first time they'd met. With a sparkle of raspberry for sweetness and something peppery for heat and below it all a sensual layer of vanilla, her scent begged him to move in close and explore every inch of her skin.

"You're right. It would be better if I left and never came back," he said, cursing the insistent thrum of hunger that made him lean in. "But that doesn't stop me from wanting to do this."

He cupped her cheek, tilting her head and caught a flash of curiosity in her autumn-toned eyes before brushing his lips across her forehead. Her body went completely still and he was pretty sure she'd stopped breathing. His own breath grew unsteady as her hands came up and clutched at his shoulders, urging him ever so slightly closer. The sheer intensity of his need to kiss her messed with his head. What power did she possess that just holding her in his arms turned him on?

He dusted kisses over her cheeks, nose and jaw, testing his willpower. Tension vibrated in her muscles but she made no move to free herself. Ryan wrapped his arm a little tighter around her, drawing her slim curves more firmly into contact with his unyielding planes and, to his delight, her lips parted on a soft moan. This was his cue and he dipped his head, sealing his lips to hers.

Time didn't just slow. It stopped. Or maybe his heart had forgotten its primary responsibility was to keep him alive. Head spinning, he lost himself in the wet, delicious slide of their lips before flicking his tongue over a bit of peppermint toothpaste that she hadn't fully rinsed away at the corner of her lips. Setting his palm against her spine, he pulled her lower half into him, letting her feel the hard ridge of his growing erection.

Her lips parted on a luxurious sigh, granting him access to her sweet mouth while her body molded to his. Ryan sent his tongue questing forward, gliding over the ridge of her teeth, taking the time to learn every curve, every taste. Despite the increased tension in both their bodies, he concentrated on each new discovery. Rushing this first kiss would be a crime. Instead he intended to savor every slow, sexy second of it. To pay attention to each shiver that buffeted her slender form and learn what she liked.

Tunneling her fingers in his hair, she met the slow thrust of his tongue like a woman who hadn't been kissed in a long time. Like someone who craved tenderness and romance.

Ryan slid his hand over her hip and down her thigh, exploring muscle and sinew. Her thin frame had deceived him into thinking she was soft and delicate. Beneath her surface lurked power. The revelation excited him. And made him realize that once again he hadn't grasped the full story.

She looped her arms around his neck, pushed up on tiptoe. The move crushed her breasts against his chest and lightning stabbed through him. Ryan groaned, the carnal sound spurring her to nip at his lower lip with an impatient growl.

He needed no further encouragement. All thoughts of taking things slow vanished. Obviously she was feeling the same sort of insistent pressure. Running his fingers through her short hair, he cupped her head and tasted her a little more deeply. Hunger stormed his body as the kiss became harder, more intense. She wobbled and gave a little moan. He shifted his hold on her, taking a firmer grip, drawing her still tighter into the carnal interplay of lips and teeth and tongue.

Somewhere as if from a great distance came the buzz and trill that signaled he had a text message. Ryan's attention jerked toward the sound, making him aware of his surroundings, the danger inherent in his loss of control and the sheer joy of letting go.

He lifted his mouth from hers, marveling at the difficulty of such a simple task. He kept his lashes lowered as he listened to his erratic breathing and wondered how big a mistake kissing her had been. At long last he peered down at Zoe, grateful to note she was equally short of breath.

"You shouldn't have done that." Despite her words and her unhappy tone, she made no attempt to free herself from his embrace.

He had his own theories on why getting involved with her was a bad idea, but was curious about her opinion on the subject. "Why not?"

His question caused her to act.

She pulled his hands from her body and held them between them. Her fingers gripped his with surprising strength. "Have you forgotten why you showed up here tonight?" she countered.

"To accuse you of lying." Even as lust continued to rage through him, Ryan welcomed the cooling tenor of her words.

"And of being on Lyle Abernathy's team."

"So our relationship has gotten off to a rocky start," he teased.

"Relationship?" She released him and stepped back out of range. "Don't get ahead of yourself. My divorce was just finalized and the last thing I'm looking for is a new man in my life."

Despite what he'd learned about her tonight, his appetite for her remained strong. As long as he remained focused on the physical chemistry between them, he could see the benefit of pursing her sexually.

His lips slid into a half smile. "Haven't you heard about rebound relationships?"

"What makes you think I haven't already had one of those? I've been separated for nearly a year."

Ryan considered her for a long moment. "I don't think so."

"Why not?" She was frowning as she asked but curiosity flickered in her eyes.

"Because you're too uptight and at the same time a powder keg of unsatisfied desire." He reached out and brushed his knuckles across her cheek. To his delight, she tipped her head and pushed into the caress. Spying a softening of her resistance, he drove his point home. "I can help you with both."

Her eyes glowed with a dreamy light but her voice had a crisp edge as she asked, "So this is a simple offer of sex?"

"Not just sex. Great sex. Let me be the bridge between your past and future."

"My Mr. Right Now?" she murmured dryly.

He smirked. "Your Mr. Anytime You Want—Any Way You Want."

Hell, if she gave him the green light, he'd carry her to the cot in the back room and screw her brains out, probably breaking things in the process.

She spent a long time scrutinizing his expression. "Can I still work for your sister's campaign?"

Her shift in topic caught him off guard. "Ah—"

"You don't trust me." When he didn't immediately deny it, she shook her head. "I can't tell if you're trying to distract me with sex or if you're just horny and looking to hook up." She surveyed him for several long seconds. "Or maybe it's both. Did you seriously think I'd be so overwhelmed with lust for you that I'd toss aside things that are important to me?"

Ryan made sure not a trace of irony showed in his smirk. "It's happened before."

"No doubt." To her credit, she didn't seem all that outraged. With noticeable force she expelled the breath from her lungs. This seemed to bolster her already robust resolve. "I think it's great, the lengths you're willing to go for your sister, but I'm not sure she'd appreciate what you're trying to do here."

She made it sound like he was making a huge sacrifice.

"Do you think I only came here because I was worried for Susannah?" In truth, as excuses went, using concern for his sister's campaign to confront Zoe was as transparent as it got. "I'm interested in you. I have been since the moment we bumped into each other. Way before anyone was suspicious enough to wonder why you'd volunteered. Does it bother me that you withheld the truth? Yes. Do I trust you? No. But that isn't enough to keep me away."

Her eyes widened, but whether at his forthright admission or his intensity, Ryan couldn't tell. He saw doubt flash across her features and wanted badly to demonstrate once again the powerful attraction between them.

"Tell me you don't feel the sexual energy between us," he continued. "That we'd be tearing each other's clothes off and rolling around on the floor if we'd met under different circumstances."

She glanced down at the pine boards and frowned. "Look—"

"Be honest," he interrupted.

"Okay," she grumbled. "There's an attraction."

With her admission, something unraveled in his chest. Ryan recognized that, given his trust issues, he'd picked the absolute wrong woman to chase after, but at the moment it didn't matter as much as it should.

"But if I ran around sleeping with all the handsome single men in Charleston," Zoe continued, "my reputation would be worse than it is right now."

"Why do you care about your reputation?"

Her brown eyes took on a haunted look. "It's all I have left."

"You can say that even after what Tristan did to you during the divorce?" He'd just tipped his hand about how much he knew about her private life, but she didn't seem at all surprised.

"Now I see why it's your sister and not you who went into politics." She turned aside and walked to the parking lot door. "Thank you for visiting. I hope you have a lovely rest of the evening."

Keeping her expression not just polite but sugar-sweet, she opened the door and the cool Charleston night air flooded the space, bringing with it the echo of distant church bells.

He moved toward her. She obviously expected him to

do the gentlemanly thing and allow himself to be shown out without further protest, but what moved through Ryan whenever he was near her had no roots in Southern manners. Instead, as he drew even with her, he caught her wrist in a gentle but firm grip. Before she knew what he intended, he lifted her hand and deposited a sizzling kiss in her palm.

"Ryan," she murmured, but whether in protest or surrender he couldn't tell. She curved her fingers against his skin and sent a soft sigh winging into the night.

Her gaze lifted to his and the air around them contracted, encasing them in a bubble where no one else existed. Ryan wasn't sure how long they remained lost in each other before the sound of a car alarm several streets over brought them back to reality.

Reluctantly, Ryan let go of her hand. The instant he set her free, she set her fingers to her lips and tore her eyes from his.

"Sweet dreams, beautiful."

And with that, he stepped into the still night.

Five

With the insistent drumbeat of anger and frustration underlying every minute of every day, Everly Briggs had a hard time spending her free time having dinner with friends or reading the latest bestseller. How could she have fun when her sister sat in jail for something that wasn't her fault?

When Kelly had first been arrested, Everly had worked tirelessly to get her sister out of trouble. In the end, however, no amount of money or willpower could keep Kelly from going to jail. And as she'd been led off after being sentenced to serving two years, shocked devastation on her face, Everly understood that while she'd failed to save her baby sister, the real blame for what had happened belonged squarely on Ryan Dailey's shoulders.

Right then and there, as her sister's sobs filled the

courtroom, Everly had determined she would do whatever it took to make him pay.

In the months following her sister's sentencing, Ryan Dailey had become her obsession. Everly had spent every free second plotting and planning. She'd researched every aspect of his life, including family and friends, spending long hours stalking him wherever he'd gone, learning his routines, contemplating all the ways she could ruin his life.

Almost immediately one thing became clear. As much as she hated to admit it, Ryan Dailey hadn't given her much to work with. Not only did his life appear impervious to meddling, his best friend was a cybersecurity specialist with friends in the Charleston PD and she didn't dare risk attacking him directly.

During the months between Kelly's arrest and her sentencing, Ryan had glimpsed Everly in the courtroom supporting her sister. Anything Everly might attempt that caused him or his sister harm would blow back in her face. That was when she'd come up with the idea of finding like-minded women with similar grievances to help her out.

Giving over control of Ryan Dailey's downfall to Zoe had been difficult, but necessary. Everly would not have chosen to partner with the former socialite. Zoe was too passive. Still, her pliancy made Zoe easy to manipulate and that was just as useful to Everly's drive for vengeance.

At the moment Everly was sitting in her car down the street from Second Chance Treasures, parked where she could see the door through which Ryan had entered the store. What was he doing visiting Zoe at this time of night? She'd been suspicious when they'd had dinner earlier, but from Zoe's tense body language as they'd said their goodbyes, the former socialite had looked uncomfortable with his interest.

Tonight when he'd showed up here, he'd been a man on a different sort of mission. His earlier flirtation had given way to anger. Everly wondered what had caused the change. Had Zoe somehow given their scheme away? If that was the case, Everly needed to formulate an alternate plan.

For days now she'd been following the political ramifications of Lyle Abernathy's entrance into the state senate race. It was well known that Abernathy was a snake. He'd stop at nothing to take down an opponent. Digging up dirt to throw Susannah Dailey-Kirby's campaign into chaos was something Everly had sent Zoe in to do. And if the pretty little former socialite couldn't handle her part? Maybe Everly could make do without her after all.

Everly was smiling over the variety of options available to her when the back door to Second Chance Treasures opened, silhouetting the couple and highlighting a disturbing tableau. Even from thirty feet away Everly recognized the chemistry that bubbled between the pair.

Rage clouded her vision for several thumping heartbeats. No. No. *No!* Ryan Dailey couldn't be allowed to seduce Zoe.

Zoe owed her allegiance to both Everly and London. Everly had ruined Linc's love life for London, who was close to securing Tristan's financial information for Zoe. Now it was up to Zoe to complete her part of the bargain.

It was imperative that Ryan Dailey be punished. Under no circumstances could he be allowed anything that might bring him joy. Especially not while Kelly was locked away because of him.

When a knock sounded on the back door less than five minutes after Ryan had left, Zoe almost didn't answer. In the wake of Ryan's kiss and the powerful emotions he'd roused in her, she was feeling shaky and raw. The idea that he might have returned for a second round of devastating kisses left Zoe filled with hope and dread.

From the moment she'd bumped into Ryan at Susannah's campaign headquarters, Zoe recognized that something about him called to her. Whether it was his knockout smile, powerful physique or the hint of wariness when he looked at her, the urge to take her clothes off and rub herself against his hard body couldn't be denied.

The knock turned to vigorous pounding and, with a grudging sigh, she went to answer. With a *what now* expression firmly in place, she swung the door open. But to her surprise, her visitor wasn't Ryan. It was so much worse.

"Have you lost your mind?" Zoe demanded of Everly Briggs, dragging the woman into the store. Shutting the door, she rounded on her. "You aren't supposed to be here. We weren't ever supposed to communicate directly with each other again. Wasn't the whole point that we're strangers who can't be connected to each other?"

"Why was Ryan Dailey here? Are you sleeping with

him?" From her narrowed eyes and accusatory tone, it was pretty obvious that Everly already believed it was the case. That she thought she had the right to demand answers fanned Zoe's temper.

"Am I sleeping with him?" After everything she'd been through tonight, this was the last straw. "What the hell are you talking about?"

"You two looked pretty cozy just now."

"What the hell, Everly?" Annoyance and apprehension battled for dominance as Zoe stared at the other woman. Not for the first time, Zoe wondered what sort of trouble she'd gotten herself into.

From their conversation at the Beautiful Women Taking Charge event Zoe had gathered that Everly had been distraught over what had happened to her sister. But they'd all been upset over their various problems. London's fiancé had given her no warning before breaking their engagement. Zoe was living through a nightmare divorce. And Everly's sister had recently gone to jail after destroying millions of dollars' worth of engineering plans.

But discovering that Everly was stalking her pushed all Zoe's buttons.

"Are you spying on me?" Zoe set her hands on her hips and gave Everly a disgusted look. "Because I really don't need to be dealing with that right now."

"No," Everly admitted. "I followed Ryan here."

With those four words Zoe recognized that Everly had issues that went far beyond her hurt and anger over what had happened to her sister.

"Why would you do that? He's not your problem,

he's mine. Honestly, what is wrong with you?" Zoe exhaled harshly and started in again before Everly could answer any of Zoe's rapid-fire questions. "I've barely started to work on the campaign. Your presence here jeopardizes everything."

Zoe could see that Everly wasn't used to being on the receiving end of a scolding and that she didn't like it one bit. Well, that was too bad. What they were doing was delicate and risky. They'd come up with a plan and, if it was to work, each of them needed to follow protocol. That meant no direct contact.

"I'm here because I need to know what's going on," Everly explained.

"That may be what you *want*," Zoe fired back, "but it's not what you *need*." She had no patience for Everly's excuses. "What you *need* is for me to fulfill my part of the bargain. Whatever that takes. If it means joining Susannah's campaign or getting friendly with Ryan, then that's what I'll do." She was breathing hard as her anger rose. "Now here's what I need. I need for you to go and not come back. Ever."

While Everly's eyes never left Zoe, her expression made it clear she wasn't focused on Zoe's lecture. "Why did he kiss your hand?"

"Did you listen to what I just said to you?" Even if she thought Everly deserved an answer, Zoe refused to explain what had happened between her and Ryan when she hadn't yet made sense of it. "You need to leave my store. Now."

"Why are you in such a hurry to get rid of me?" Everly demanded. "Is he coming back?"

"Haven't you understood anything I've said?" Her righteous anger felt satisfying and powerful.

"I understand that you want me to go," Everly said, the fervent light in her eyes convincing Zoe that the woman was unbalanced. "But I'm not leaving until I'm satisfied with your answers."

"I don't owe you any explanations," Zoe responded even though she could see her words fell on deaf ears.

"That's where you're wrong. You do owe me. And you owe London. We're all in this together."

"Look, I didn't interfere with what you did to Linc or with London going after Tristan." That the latter scheme might still blow up terrified Zoe too much for her to risk showing any involvement. "You need to back off and let me handle this."

"Are you sleeping with him?"

"No."

"No not ever or no not yet?" Everly was a dog with a bone.

"Listen," Zoe said, nearing the end of her patience. "I'm playing him any way I can. Now I really need you to leave." She walked to the door and opened it.

When Everly didn't move, Zoe wondered if she'd have to get physical. As much as the idea of wrestling Everly out the door appealed to Zoe, neither one of them could afford the attention a catfight might attract.

"Fine," Everly snarled. "But I'm going to keep an eye on both of you. If for one second I think that you're betraying me, you're going to be sorry."

Zoe shivered at Everly's threat, recognizing the wisdom in treading carefully. Tristan had a temper like that. It burned slow and white-hot and, as she'd learned, with devastating results.

"I'm not going to betray you," Zoe said, "but you have to stay far away from me. Ryan knows who you are and if he sees us together, everything will be ruined."

"He won't see us together."

"You don't know that. He doesn't trust me," Zoe said in her most mild and reasonable tone. "That's why he came by tonight. To accuse me of lying to him and to find out if I'm a spy for Lyle Abernathy. It's possible that he's having me watched." Zoe doubted it was the case, but her words fed Everly's paranoia. Noting that Everly continued to hesitate, Zoe drove the point home. "After all, you're keeping tabs on him."

The wild light in Everly's eyes dimmed somewhat. "Okay, I see your point."

"Good. Now go home and get some sleep." Zoe gestured Everly out and, to her relief, the woman stepped into the parking lot. "I've got this handled."

Without answering, Everly marched toward the far side of the lot where a dark Audi sedan was parked.

Zoe sighed as she closed and locked the door.

For three days Ryan kept his distance from Zoe while he processed all he'd learned about her background. He avoided the campaign headquarters when he knew she was volunteering and resisted the temptation to stop into Second Chance Treasures to say hello.

But he couldn't stop his thoughts from lingering on the memory of their kiss or dwelling on the foolish longing to learn about her childhood and the sort of music she enjoyed.

Yesterday he'd sent her a text, reminding her about their Saturday night date. She'd tried to convince him to let her meet him at the restaurant where they were eating, but now that he knew where she lived, he intended to pick her up. If he told her they were eating at his place, he doubted she'd come. And she'd be right to resist. He intended to lull her with expensive wine and delicious food before encouraging her to spill all her secrets.

Ryan parked near the back door of Zoe's store and glanced at the time. He was five minutes early. An uncomfortable anxiety gripped him as he exited the car and went to collect her. When was the last time going on a date with a woman had made him nervous? The answer disturbed him as much as the turmoil in his gut. Never. His reaction to Zoe was unique in his life.

Ryan knew part of his disquiet was based on a decision he'd made earlier that day. The wisdom of it utterly escaped him, but he was starting to realize that his behavior when it came to Zoe deviated from logic.

She answered the door casually dressed in a gray sweater and slim jeans. Her gaze roved over him; his jeans and white button-down shirt were similarly casual. She frowned.

"You look beautiful," he remarked, glad he'd shoved his hands into his pockets before she'd appeared. After being apart from her these last few days, the need to kiss her had grown stronger.

"Where are we headed?"

"It's a surprise."

"I don't like surprises."

"Not even good ones?"

She lapsed into silence and let him escort her to the passenger side of his car.

The drive to his house took less than ten minutes. She looked relaxed and calm as he guided the car down King Street, but the minute he turned onto an obvious residential avenue, she sat straighter.

"Where are we going?"

"Dinner."

"Yes, but where?"

"My house." He glanced in her direction as he slowed and parked beside the curb. "A friend of mine planned a wonderful menu especially for us."

"This is yours?" She stared at the house. "Funny, you don't strike me as a Queen Anne."

"The inside is more modern." Suddenly he was eager to show it off.

She looked concerned. "Not too modern, I hope."

"You'll see."

The full tour took them nearly thirty minutes. Ryan paid careful attention to her every expression as she strolled through the rooms, missing none of the crown moldings or the wood inlays in the living- and dining-room floors. Her eyebrows rose as she assessed his minimalist styling, modern light fixtures and enormous upstairs bedrooms.

"Come outside and see the pool," he coaxed, drawing her onto the back porch.

"This is really beautiful back here. How big is the lot?"

"A quarter acre."

"That's big for downtown Charleston."

"Come this way. I have something else to show you."
He led the way along the porch to the first of his guest
apartments. "The previous owners created two one-bedroom units back here that they leased out. I use them
when family or friends come from out of town." He
opened the first door and gestured her inside.

"This is nice," Zoe commented, her gaze sweeping
over the open galley kitchen, cozy navy sofa and high
ceilings. "I imagine your guests enjoy the separate space."

"It's yours for as long as you need it."

"What?" She gaped at him.

"Most of the time the apartment is empty. I'd like for
you to stay here until you can get back on your feet."

She made a series of faces as she thought it over
but it was obvious she was tempted. At long last she
sighed. "I can't."

"Why not?"

"Whatever you're charging, I can't afford it."

"I'm not charging you anything."

"But you don't know me. And may I remind you that
earlier this week you were accusing me of working for
the opposition."

"I talked to Susannah and told her I believed you
could be trusted."

The morning following their dinner at Bertha's
Kitchen, he'd met with his sister and Gil, passing on
everything that he'd learned. Susannah had been satisfied, but Gil hadn't been ready to give up so easily.
Several run-ins with Abernathy over the years had left
him very suspicious.

"What if I move in and get so comfortable I never move out?" Zoe continued, her arguments growing more desperate.

"I doubt you're going to do that."

"You don't know me," she repeated, but with less vigor this time.

"So, let's go have dinner and you can fill me in."

Ryan had no idea if she was giving his offer serious consideration as they settled in the dining room. His table was large enough to accommodate ten, but Ryan wanted a more intimate meal so he had set two places on one end. With the lights of his modern chandelier dimmed to romantic levels and candles flickering, the mood was intimate and relaxed.

"This is quite nice," Zoe commented vaguely, her expression unreadable as she sipped a chilled glass of crisp white wine and glanced around.

"Do I make you nervous?" he asked, sensing the ambience wasn't having its desired effect.

"Yes."

As much as he wanted to grill her, Ryan held silent, hoping she'd fill the emptiness with explanations.

"It's all a bit much, don't you think?"

He shook his head. "I'm not sure I understand what you mean."

"The offer to move into your house. The romantic dinner." She leaned back in her chair and regarded him. "I feel as if you're an advancing hurricane and I waited too long to evacuate."

"You need a place to stay. I have one. I like helping people."

"So your sister mentioned a few days ago." Zoe cocked her head. "She said you tried to help someone last year and it led to the trouble at your company."

Ryan's gut clenched and he gave a tight nod. "Kelly Briggs was a disturbed young woman."

"She cost you millions."

"Yes."

"And yet you don't know me at all and you're willing to help me out." Her eyes drilled into him as she searched for answers. "What if the same thing happens again?"

"Will it?"

Before she could answer, they were interrupted by the arrival of the first course delivered by Paul's cousin. Dallas Shaw had worked for several upscale Charleston restaurants over the years. She was currently a private chef looking for investors so she could open her own restaurant.

The redhead smiled as she set the plates down and began her presentation. "What I have for you to start is smoked salmon toast with petite arugula and cucumber salad. Enjoy."

"This looks wonderful," Zoe murmured, taking a bite, her eyes going wide with pleasure.

As he watched her savor the appetizer one delicate bite at a time, Ryan realized how much he wanted to make her happy. She'd obviously had a hard time in the last year, but instead of whining about it, she'd dug in and tried to improve her situation. His family valued hard work.

"Earlier you said you want to know more about me,"

Zoe said, her grim tone making her sound like a suspect sitting in an interrogation room. "Where should I start?"

"Wherever you wish."

Zoe waited until Dallas replaced the appetizer plates with a beet and pistachio salad before declaring, "Tristan accused me of infidelity as the reason he wanted a divorce."

Shock stabbed Ryan. "You cheated on your husband?"

Her lips twitched in amusement at his sharp reaction. "No, but Tristan made it look as if I had."

"How did he do that?"

"He paid someone to falsify a paper trail and doctor photos. You can make anything look real if you throw enough resources at it."

It struck Ryan then how cynical she was. And damaged. Her ex had done a number on her. Red flags began to flutter in his mind and he decided to ask Paul what he knew about Tristan Crosby.

"But in your case the truth won out," Ryan said.

Zoe's eyes reflected a deep and profound sadness as she said, "Sure, but this town is all about appearances and doubts will linger long after the real story comes out."

She wasn't wrong, and it irritated Ryan how often gossip trumped truth. His parents had emphasized fair play would take the twins farther than cutting corners or cheating. Because not everyone subscribed to the same lofty values, sometimes doing the right thing didn't mean you were going to win.

"A week from today there's a fund-raising dinner

for Susannah at the Whitney Plantation," Ryan said. "I agreed to go, but I don't have a date."

"Do you need one?"

Ryan wondered if she was being deliberately obtuse. Didn't the woman realize he'd brought it up because he wanted her to accompany him?

"It gets old always being the third wheel around my sister and her husband," Ryan said. "They are the perfect couple."

"It must be terrible for you being the eligible bachelor all the time."

"You have no idea," Ryan told her. "Will you be my date for the evening?"

She gnawed on her lower lip as she gave the invitation some thought. "I haven't gone to any events where I might run into…people from my former life," she murmured, taking a sip of wine.

"It would be a great opportunity to promote your store," he said, hoping that would be enough to entice her. "And I'll be there to look out for you."

"It seems like I should say yes then," she replied with a slow smile.

"Good."

For the rest of the meal they stuck to easy topics like tourist attractions around Charleston neither one had visited and favorite area beaches. Ryan spoke about growing up as a twin and discovered Zoe had three older sisters who lived all over the country. Two were married with children and one worked on Wall Street.

He was finishing the last bit of chocolate hazelnut mousse when Zoe gave a huge sigh. Unsure what had prompted such a dramatic sound, Ryan glanced her way. To his surprise, her eyes were filled with tears.

"I'm really tired of sleeping in the back room of the store," she announced in a shaky voice.

"I imagine you are," he said, his heartbeat a hard thump against his ribs as he watched her dab at the corners of her eyes with her napkin. "Let's finish our wine and go get your stuff."

The limited number of things Zoe owned was brought home in a big way as Ryan regarded the two suitcases she rolled toward the back door of the shop.

"Is that everything?" he asked, making no effort to hide his surprise.

She hiked a large tote onto her shoulder and nodded. "I didn't take much when Tristan evicted me from our house on Daniel Island. If I'd been less shell-shocked, I might've grabbed more than just some essentials, two suitcases full of clothes and the few pieces of jewelry he let me take." As she spoke, her expression twisted with embarrassment and regret. "Everything was in his name. The cars. The house. My credit cards. I left the house the same way I'd arrived, owning nothing except what he'd given me." She paused a beat before finishing, "And what he gave, he could also take away."

That she continued to open up about things that had bothered her a great deal gave Ryan hope that she was feeling more comfortable with him by the moment. Hearing the pain in her voice helped him understand why she'd been so cagey about her past.

Moving her into the guest apartment took less than

ten minutes. Sensing that she still needed some time to adjust to her new situation and surroundings, he left her to explore the space and returned to the main house.

As he was heading upstairs, Ryan noticed that Paul had tried to reach him while they'd been at the store and he called him back. "Hey," he said when his friend picked up. "What's up?"

He moved to the double window in the master bedroom that overlooked the backyard. The pool glowed a bright turquoise below.

"Sorry I haven't gotten back to you sooner about that store you wanted me to look into, but one of my cases heated up in the last few days."

"No problem," Ryan said, figuring he already knew what Paul had learned. "Were you able to find out anything interesting?"

"Zoe Alston owns Second Chance Treasures," Paul said, confirming what she'd already admitted. "The building is owned by Dillworth Properties."

"Dillworth Properties," Ryan repeated, the name a faint whisper in his memory. Something about it made him uneasy, but he couldn't place the reason. "Why does that sound familiar?"

"Because it's owned by George Dillworth."

Ryan cursed. "As in Lyle Abernathy's oldest and dearest friend."

"That's it. Also, I did a little checking. She's three months behind on her lease, but so far they haven't shown any signs of evicting her."

She'd mentioned having financial difficulties, but three months was a long time to go without paying rent.

"How much does she owe?" Ryan asked.

"Fifteen thousand."

He rubbed at his temples as a dull ache began to throb there. "That might be enough to make her desperate. It wouldn't surprise me if Abernathy took advantage of her situation."

"I was thinking the same thing."

Neither man spoke for a long moment, giving Ryan an opportunity to ponder how to handle this new revelation.

At last Paul spoke again. "What are you going to do?"

"I can't confront her about it. She won't appreciate that I'm still having her investigated."

"So what's left?"

Ryan hesitated a beat. "I'd already decided the best way to keep an eye on her was to stick as close as possible."

"How close is that?" Paul asked, his voice a blend of curiosity and amusement.

"I moved her into one of my guest apartments."

"That's awfully close. Are you sure it's a good idea?"

"Probably not, but she was sleeping in the back of her store because she ran out of money." And Ryan was banking on proximity fanning the sparks between them into flame. "You know, if Abernathy is using her financial problems to put pressure on her to dig up dirt on Susannah, then maybe I can take away his leverage."

"And how do you plan to do that?"

"By making an anonymous payment to Dillworth Properties on behalf of her store."

"You know this is all speculation and there might not be anything going on," Paul pointed out, his level tone giving no hint of his opinion. "You could be throwing money away for no good reason."

Ryan considered that, but whatever Zoe was mixed up in, he had faith that when it came to the women she was trying to help, her heart was pure.

"I give to charity all the time," Ryan pointed out. "This is no different."

Except that this cause was acutely personal to him.

"And," he added, "we still don't know if she's at all connected to Abernathy."

"Do you want me to keep digging?"

"Thanks for the offer, but I think you've spent more than enough time indulging my paranoia."

Ryan hung up and considered what he'd just learned. Although the news brought back the demons of distrust, he realized that even though he still had questions about her motivations, his suspicions, potent though they might be, weren't enough to stop him from wanting her.

A voice in his head reminded him that he'd known Zoe for little more than a week, but a drumbeat of lust and longing held more sway. He felt a connection with her that outstripped anything he'd ever experienced before. He simply couldn't let her go until she'd worked her way out of his system. Whatever that took.

Six

For the last week, Zoe had been staying in Ryan's guest apartment. Each morning that she woke up in the king-size bed and shuffled into the open-concept kitchen, dining and living space with its high ceilings and heart-pine floors, the hardships of the last year faded a little more. And it wasn't just her new environment having a positive effect on her psyche, but also the amount of time she'd been spending with her handsome landlord that lent her optimism a gigantic boost.

The night after she'd moved in, he'd appeared at her door at six.

"Hungry?" he'd asked.

She'd gone out earlier and stocked her refrigerator, but hadn't decided on what to make for dinner. "I guess."

"I'm about to throw something on the barbecue," he said, not seeming at all put off by her ambivalence. "And I hate eating alone."

"Me, too."

Though she'd gotten used to it, being married to Tristan. He often worked late. Or at least that was the excuse he'd given on the nights he'd come home late smelling of perfume and red wine.

"I'll throw together a salad and come over."

That dinner became the first of many. Every night Ryan would stop by her door with an invite, sometimes still dressed in his tailored suits, other times in jeans and a T-shirt. Every night she said yes because being with him was so much fun. With Ryan she laughed and argued and felt utterly normal.

He possessed exactly what she needed to make the world go away. Or at least to enable her to forget all about it for a while. His smile kindled a glow in her chest. The glancing contact with his body as they worked side by side left her giddy and breathless. His fingers tantalized her skin as he caressed her cheek or held her hand. And when his lips closed over hers at the end of the evening, stealing her sighs and setting her blood on fire, she couldn't imagine being happier.

Tonight's dinner was different from the last few. Instead of fixing a meal together in Ryan's big, white kitchen, he was taking her on a double date with Susannah and Jefferson. Everything in her rebelled against getting in deeper with the Dailey siblings because the more time she spent with them, the harder it would be to do them harm. And she was starting to wonder if there was anything to dig up concerning Susannah or her campaign.

What if it was impossible to come up with something? That sure wouldn't make Everly happy and her erratic behavior the night Ryan had come by the store left Zoe convinced the woman might do something disastrous.

Pushing aside the problem of Everly's unwanted intervention for the moment, Zoe turned her attention to another bit of trouble. She picked up the envelope that had arrived in the mail today. For weeks now she'd been expecting something from the property management company telling her that she had to vacate. She was three months behind on the rent and it was only a matter of time before they kicked her out.

With a heavy sigh, Zoe slit open the envelope and pulled out the invoice from Dillworth Properties. She smoothed the sheet of paper and braced herself for the total at the bottom.

The number was zero.

How was that possible? She owed fifteen thousand dollars.

Zoe pulled out her phone and dialed the number of the management company. When the receptionist answered, she asked to speak to Tom Gossett.

"Tom, it's Zoe Alston," she began, her voice vibrating with anxiety. "I just received my monthly invoice and it looks like there's been a mistake."

"Oh?" Tom was in his midfifties and had a calm, methodical way about him. "How so?"

"It shows that I don't owe you any money when I'm sure that I'm three months behind."

"Well," he said, chuckling. "I'm pretty sure I've never had a tenant call to complain that they didn't owe us any money."

Zoe bit her lip, not finding the situation at all funny. "I don't understand what's going on. I know I haven't sent you any money."

"Well, someone did." The sound of computer keys clicking came over the phone. "I show a payment coming into our office two days ago."

"Are you sure it was for my store?"

"I have a copy of the cashier's check in your file. It says Second Chance Treasures on it. That's your store, right?"

"Yes." Zoe felt light-headed. Who could possibly have done something like that? "I can't believe this happened."

"Believe it. Is there anything else?"

"No. Thank you."

Zoe hung up the phone and clasped her shaking hands together. She didn't know whether to laugh or cry. On the one hand, the incredible gesture relieved a huge burden and left her feeling as if someone in this world cared about her well-being. It also meant she could move forward with a nearly clean slate. The store could stay open. She could continue her crusade to help victims of domestic violence. On the other hand, the fact that she'd needed to be bailed out filled her with shame and anger.

And the fact that the payment's origin was a mystery bothered her. Who knew exactly how much she owed? The answer struck her a second later. She'd mentioned to Ryan that she was behind on the rent, not so that he'd help, but because she'd grown comfortable enough with him that she'd begun to share some of her fears as well as her hopes.

Had Ryan made the anonymous payment? He'd already demonstrated his helpfulness when he'd given her a place to live rent-free. But offering an empty apartment was different from shelling money out of his pocket. And why hadn't he been upfront and offered her a loan? Because he knew she wouldn't have taken the money?

Instead he'd snuck around behind her back?

And done something incredibly nice.

Meanwhile she was plotting to destroy his sister. How could she blithely accept his help while actively working to cause him harm?

Ryan had texted to say he was running a bit late, giving Zoe even more time to stew and fret about confronting him. As the afternoon had worn on, she'd changed her mind a dozen times about how to approach the subject. Outrage and appreciation went hand in hand as she'd reimagined her budget, finding ways to economize so she could repay him.

But all her judicious statements vanished as she opened her front door and spied him standing on the side porch, looking confident and authoritative in a blue-plaid blazer, gray slacks and white dress shirt. He looked relaxed, elegant and so happy to see her.

Zoe's heart clenched, driving tears of frustration to her eyes.

"Damn it, Ryan," she protested, wanting badly to feel either one way or another about him.

Angry. Happy. Hate. Love. Desire. Disgust.

Emotions swirled through her in a complicated tornado, moving too fast for her to latch onto just one.

"What's the matter?" He frowned in confusion. "I texted and told you I was going to be late."

"That's not the problem," she muttered, flashing the invoice she'd received from Dillworth Properties. "This is the problem. Did you do this?"

He took the paper from her and scanned it. "Looks like your rent is current. Congratulations."

"It's current because someone paid my rent for me. Was it you?"

For several heartbeats he looked as if he wasn't going to answer truthfully, but he must have recognized she'd already decided he was responsible and wouldn't let the matter drop.

"I know how worried you were about losing your lease and having to close the store."

Although she'd expected his confession, she was stunned. What was he thinking? Days earlier he'd regarded her with suspicion. Now he was bailing out her store?

She didn't ask him why he'd done it. His sympathetic expression illuminated his motives. He'd been trying to help her out. But the way he'd gone about it made her failure so much more acute. And how could she accept money from him when her purpose in getting close to him was to cause him and his sister harm? Contradictory forces tore at Zoe, making it hard for her to breathe.

"I'm going to pay you back every penny," she said, fighting to lift her voice above a whisper. "It's going to take me a while, but the store's doing better every single month."

"You don't have to pay me back," he replied, returning the invoice. "Consider it a donation to your cause."

Zoe's hands balled into fists. Admitting she couldn't afford to turn enough of a profit to support her dream roused her shame. Through their entire marriage, every time Tristan had given her money, she'd surrendered her independence and damaged her self-worth.

"Second Chance Treasures isn't a charity," she shot back, her pride rallying. "And neither am I."

"That's not at all what I thought." He caught her hand and gave a reassuring squeeze. "I just wanted to help out a friend."

Zoe fought the calm that filled her whenever he was around. She couldn't just let him soothe her concerns. "But you did it anonymously."

"So you didn't have to worry about paying me back."

"I can't just take your money," she countered, recognizing as much as she wanted to make it on her own, the awful truth was that she would've eventually been out on the street without his help.

"Are you really going to be this stubborn? If one of your friends had given you the money with no expectations of getting it back, would you be digging your heels in?"

What friends? The sardonic question was on the tip of her tongue, but she held it back.

"Please understand that being able to make it on my own is very important to me," she said quietly. "I appreciate your help, but I wish you'd offered me a loan or told me what you were going to do."

"My actions might have been a little heavy-handed. Susannah is often telling me that I run roughshod over people when I try to help." He pulled her forward and wrapped his arms around her. "What can I do to fix it? If you want, I can call Dillworth Properties and get my money back."

At his mocking tone, Zoe jabbed her knuckles into his ribs hard enough that he winced. "I spent some time looking at my books today and I think I can pay you back over the next six months."

Ryan stepped back and cupped her face in his hands. He lowered his lips to hers and kissed her with great energy, snatching her breath away and making her head spin. Lust surged and she gave herself over to it, even as he backed off before things heated up too much. Once again his control awakened her anxiety. Didn't he want to have sex with her?

Even as the question popped into her head, Zoe cringed. Not only had they only known each other a week, but there was this little matter of her role in the revenge bargain she'd made with Everly and London. But every moment in his company drove her libido into the red zone. She craved his hands on her and took every opportunity to bring her body into contact with his. Although she could see he recognized her not-so-subtle signals, he had yet to act.

She told herself to be grateful for his restraint even as she swooned against him, surrendering her mouth to the masterful pressure of his lips and sweep of his tongue. Moving forward into deeper intimacy with Ryan would only intensify her already complicated battle between what she wanted and what she'd promised to do.

Oblivious to her inner struggles, Ryan kissed his

way toward her cheek to whisper in her ear. "Take a year if you need it." His statement ended in a grunt as her knuckles connected with his ribs a second time. "Okay. Okay. Six months is perfect," he amended, his tone teasing. "And I think ten percent interest should be just about right." He caught her hand before she could strike again and dusted a kiss across her knuckles. "You know I'm kidding about the interest, right?"

She nodded, her throat tight with overwhelming gratitude at the easing of her immediate financial concerns.

"Good." He smiled down at her. "Now, we're going to be late for our reservation if we don't get going."

"Enough stories about my ill-spent youth," Ryan groused fondly, interrupting his sister and Zoe, who were laughing at his expense. "Talk to Susannah about your store and all the women you're helping."

With a glance his way, Susannah sobered. "Ryan mentioned you had a boutique in downtown Charleston that is doing great work with victims of domestic violence. He said they make things that you sell."

Zoe's eyes glowed as she launched into her story. Watching her friendship with his sister develop over cocktails and crab cakes was exactly what Ryan had hoped for this evening. Susannah was such a huge part of his life and her approval was more than important. It was imperative.

His perspective had shifted over the last week while he'd gotten to know Zoe better. Moving her into his guest apartment meant that he was no longer thinking of her in terms of someone he intended to hook up with and move on. He enjoyed having her around. The more time they spent together, the more she opened up, and he was discovering she suited him quite well.

Standing in the way of that were his seesawing concerns whether or not she was a spy for Lyle Abernathy. Which demonstrated that he didn't fully trust her. Nor was he sure what it would take until she was completely above suspicion. It frustrated him that he couldn't move their relationship forward while his first thought was to question her motives.

When they'd arrived at the table, they'd settled in with the women on one side and the men on the other. The seating arrangement and the way the women took to each other had made it challenging for the men to stay engaged in their conversation. Now, with Zoe and Susannah engrossed in a discussion about Second Chance Treasures, Ryan glanced toward his brother-in-law and found him texting.

"So, Jefferson, how're things going with you?"

The innocuous question startled his brother-in-law into slamming his phone facedown on the table and snatching up his drink. A flush crept up his neck as he answered.

"You know. Business is good. Family is fine."

Ryan eyed Jefferson and wondered why the guy was so jumpy. "How is it with Susannah on the campaign trail? I suppose you're busier than ever with the kids' activities."

"That's for sure." From beside his plate came a buzzing sound and Jefferson's gaze shot to his phone. "Between Violet's dance lessons and Casey's soccer games, it feels like all we do is run."

The buzz came again. And a muscle in Jefferson's jaw worked.

"Sounds like someone is eager to get hold of you," Ryan commented, wondering why his brother-in-law seemed so on edge. "Go ahead and answer if you need to."

"It's fine."

A third buzz sounded and a thin layer of sweat formed on Jefferson's brow. "Ah, maybe I'll just step outside and see what's going on. My mom's trying to coordinate Thanksgiving dinner with my sister and her family..." Trailing off, he snagged his phone and got to his feet. "I'll be back in a couple minutes."

Ryan watched him go with a sense of uneasiness before his attention was caught by the women's conversation across the table.

"I'll talk to Gil to make sure we can fit it in the schedule, but I think it would be a great idea," Susannah said.

"What would?" Ryan interjected.

"Susannah is going to come talk at one of our Wednesday night events at the store."

"See," Ryan said to Zoe, "I knew my sister would be interested in helping you out."

"We're helping out each other," his sister corrected, her gaze lingering on Jefferson's empty seat. "Does anyone want this last shrimp? Otherwise I'm going to eat it."

After dinner the two couples parted ways with Susannah insisting they needed to head home to relieve the babysitter. Ryan was happy to cut the evening short. He was interested in some alone time with Zoe.

"That was more fun than I expected," she said on the way to his house. "Your sister is very different away from the campaign."

"Susannah has two personalities. Private and public. It's grown even more pronounced since she decided to run for office. Tonight you saw little of the mischief-maker I grew up with. She can be pretty unrestrained at home."

"I enjoyed hearing stories about you growing up."

"I assure you only ten percent of what she told you was true."

"Only ten percent?" Doubt salted Zoe's voice. "I'd guess more like fifty or sixty percent."

"Notice I didn't return the favor," Ryan muttered as he pulled into his garage. "I have stories about my sister that would change your opinion of her."

"You showed great restraint," Zoe replied.

"Do you want to come in for a while?" Ryan reached out and ran his fingers lightly over her knee. "It's too early to call it a night."

Her voice was a little breathless as she answered. "Sure."

As they walked hand-in-hand along the side porch, Ryan's anticipation reached a feverish point. He barely managed to close the back door before he backed her up against his kitchen wall.

"I can't wait any longer," he murmured, bracing his arm beside her head so he could lean in. "I have to kiss you."

"Just kiss?" she murmured, peering at him from beneath her long lashes.

When surprise made him slow to respond, hot color flooded her cheeks.

"Do you want to do more?" he asked, his voice thick and dark with hunger.

Her hands coasted around his waist and up his back. "That's been my hope for days now."

"How much more?"

She lifted on tiptoe and pressed her lips to his ear. "I want to get naked with you," she whispered, her breath sliding over his skin.

He groaned. "Baby, you have no idea how good it is to hear you say that."

She gasped in surprise when he scooped her off her feet and carried her into the living room. He lowered her to the couch before settling his weight onto her. She stretched beneath him and gave a sexy little murmur that lit up his body like a fireworks finale.

Cupping her cheek, he brushed his thumb over her full lower lip. He wanted to make what came next good for her. That meant taking things slow and making sure their lovemaking offered mutual combustion.

"Zoe," he whispered, his heart racing as she clutched his shoulders.

"Yes, Ryan?"

"I'm gonna make this really good for you."

Her smile was like dawn breaking over Charleston Harbor. "You know you don't need to worry about me."

He blinked. Had she actually just said that? "Baby, you can't stop me from putting your needs first."

At his declaration, she glanced away, but not before he spied a glint of moisture in her eyes.

"Thank you."

His chest tightened. Such simple words, but her tone was poignant with surprise and relief. The urge to find her ex-husband and punch the living crap out of him burned in his gut.

Ryan drew in a long, slow, steady breath and pushed all thoughts of anger or violence to the back of his mind.

Her fingers slid into his hair as he dropped his head and lowered his lips to hers. He wanted to start slow and let the passion build at a measured pace, but her hands skimmed over his shoulder and ribs, fingers digging into his skin as her lips parted and a hungry moan erupted from her throat.

Suddenly, holding back was beyond his control. His desire for her had been building since the moment she'd bumped into him at Susannah's campaign office.

Ryan swept his tongue around hers, deepening the kiss, reveling in the raw hunger with which she kissed him back. In that moment he knew he could never get enough of her. Of the give-and-take between them. Of her passion. Her taste. The way her nails dug into his back and her teeth nipped at his lower lip.

For several seconds her ferocity surprised him. There was always something so reserved and guarded about the way she spoke and moved. Who would've guessed all this unruliness bubbled beneath her watchful eyes and careful expressions?

"Tell me what you like," she whispered.

"How about I show you instead."

Seven

Ryan's words sent a cascade of happiness through Zoe. For days she'd been imagining this moment, but nothing she'd dreamed up had come close to the thrill of Ryan's hard body pressing her into the cushions. She bent her knee and the fabric of his slacks scraped against her sensitive inner thigh. Every nerve ending cried out for the touch of his skin on hers.

She'd worn her sexiest underwear tonight and a wrap dress that came undone with a simple tug. She hadn't wanted buttons or zippers to get in the way of his hands finding her naked flesh. Unfortunately, with his weight bearing down on her, she couldn't get free of her clothes. The frustration made her groan.

"You smell delicious," he murmured, trailing soft

kisses down her neck. "It was the second thing I noticed about you."

"What was the first?" she asked.

"Your eyes," he told her. "They were the most amazing color I'd ever seen."

"I noticed that your hands were strong and also gentle. It made me wonder what it would be like to have them all over my body."

Setting her foot on the couch, she shifted her position until he slid into the V between her thighs. He was now in a much better position for her to get some relief from the ache pulsing between her legs.

She bumped her hips against his, rocking the most sensitive part of her against the hard ridge straining his zipper. The move caused him to release a husky groan. He slid his hand over her butt, pulling her hard against him.

"Do that again," he commanded, his fingertip skimming beneath her silk panties.

This time when she repeated the move, she gave her hips a little twist and his fingers grazed close enough to where she so desperately craved his touch that she whimpered.

She slid her fingers into his hair and imagined all the sexy, dirty things she was going to do to him. Sex with Tristan hadn't always been about romance or even passion. Sometimes she'd felt anonymous beneath him. Especially when he'd flip her onto her stomach and take her from behind. At that moment she could've been anyone to him. It hadn't occurred to her at first. She'd been a virgin on her wedding night, having never experimented with boys her own age. Which meant that a man who was eleven years her senior, with a lot more life experience, could convince her that whatever he told her was the truth.

And it wasn't as if she had friends she could reach out to about the subject. She'd run with a similarly sheltered group of women who'd pledged virginity until marriage. Nor could she speak to her mother about such a subject. Helena Alston was a soft-spoken, Southern gentlewoman who would be scandalized to discuss such private bedroom matters.

Later, when Zoe had established herself in society and gained some confidence, she'd realized that asking questions of her peers about their intimate moments would only point out her naïveté and open her up to ridicule. Since maintaining appearances was so important to Tristan, she'd hesitated to say or to do anything that might leave anyone questioning his ability to satisfy a woman in bed.

One thing he had done was teach her how to please a man, something she was about to demonstrate to Ryan. Even more, possibly for the first time ever, she wanted to give pleasure. And Ryan was the target of all those persistent impulses.

Her heart was pattering way too fast and none too steadily. What if she couldn't please him? Almost as soon as the thought speared her mind, she felt strong fear dig in.

"Look," Ryan began, obviously reading uncertainty in her hesitation. He ran his thumb over her cheek. "We don't have to do this."

Oh, hell no. He wasn't getting away that easily.

"I need to do this," she explained, her focus centered on the hard bulge pressed against her.

"'Need'?" he repeated, his voice reflecting concern. "You don't need to do anything. Let me take care of you."

He lifted his hand and ran the tips of his fingers over her cheek. The tender gesture made tears spring to her eyes. Talk about a mood killer. Crying a bucket of tears onto a man's erection wasn't exactly sexy.

"I...*want* to do this." She stressed the second word, making herself sound powerful and confident. And it was the truth. "Kiss me," she begged, loving that he knew exactly what she liked best. Hard and soft. Tender and hungry. In his arms her senses came alive and she adored every second.

"My pleasure."

As his mouth settled over hers, she crushed her lips to his. This man turned her on and she wanted him to know it. A deep, sexy rumble of pleasure sounded from his throat. He curved his fingers over her waist and rode the bumps of her ribs to her breast. As his palm covered her, she whimpered with joy.

"You are so beautiful," he murmured against her neck, his teeth raking across her throat. "I can't get enough of you."

Zoe gripped his hair and gave a sharp yelp as he tweaked her nipple through her clothing. She saw his half smile as he lowered his mouth to her breast. As her blood pounded in her ears, she almost missed his appreciative groan when her nipple tightened against his tongue.

A curse slipped from her lips. The sensation of his mouth on her breast was blunted by the fabric that separated them.

"This isn't working," she protested, tugging at his hair.

He lifted his head and gave her a wicked smile. "Could've fooled me."

"We're both wearing too many clothes."

"I know." But he didn't seem immediately inclined to tear her clothes off.

His mouth drifted across her chest to her other breast and her thoughts turned to ash as a jolt of pure lust blasted through her. He hooked his fingers in her neckline and pulled both her dress and bra aside so he could flick his tongue over her nipple.

"Oh, yes," she murmured, a cry lodging in her throat as fire swept through her. "So good."

She held him against her as he plied her with lips, teeth and tongue. Meanwhile the insistent drumbeat of hunger grew louder and faster. She was burning up and gyrating beneath him on the couch wasn't getting her anywhere near where she wanted to go.

"Take me upstairs," she demanded, pushing her hips into his hand as he eased his way down her body until his shoulders shifted between her knees, pushing them wider.

He dragged his finger over her panties and cursed. "You're so wet."

She squeaked something incoherent as he pressed a

kiss over her clit. White-hot lightning shot through her, leaving Zoe panting and trembling.

"And so gorgeous," Ryan continued. "I love the way you smell and can't wait to find out how you taste."

His words were almost as arousing as the firm grip he took on her panties. With a sudden tug, he shifted them off her hips and down her legs. The damp fabric hadn't done much to shield her most intimate self, but as he stripped away the silk underwear, Zoe's sudden exposure made her tremble.

With her underwear no longer a barrier between them, Ryan lay between her thighs and slid a finger along the landing strip that led to the heart of her. While her body vibrated with sharp longing, he seemed content to slow down and take his time.

Zoe closed her eyes as he grazed his fingers along the folds that hid her sex from him. As he dipped ever so delicately into her slick heat, she arched into his touch. Was he toying with her? Did he want her to beg? Because she was ready to say whatever he wanted to hear if only he would make the ache go away.

"Please," she pleaded, nearly incoherent as he continued his gentle exploration. "I need more."

"My tongue?"

Now he was understanding her. "Yes," she breathed, light-headed with relief. "I need your mouth on me. Now!"

"Like this?"

He flicked his tongue against her swollen clit and the noise that erupted out of her was like a mad keen. The pleasure felt so intense and perfect.

"Oh, yes! More like that."

His deep chuckle echoed through her body, intensifying the hum of anticipation flowing through her. He sounded so pleased with her answer that despite the tension locked in her muscles, she felt a sudden rush of joy. In that instant she knew it was going to be good between them. Better than she'd ever known. Ryan was going to take care of her.

Gratitude made her heart clench, but she barely had a chance to register the emotion because a second later the only thing she knew was a white-hot blaze of desire as Ryan spread her legs wider and sent his tongue into her heat.

In an instant she was lost. In the man. In her need. In their desire as she rocked her hips and groaned his name. Distantly she heard her name as well as some deliciously erotic murmurings from Ryan's lips.

He made her feel sexy. Letting go during sex was about trusting her partner enough to be vulnerable and for most of her marriage Zoe hadn't known what to expect from her husband. Ryan was a completely different story and her body reacted accordingly. Pleasure coiled tighter and tighter inside her so fast she barely recognized what was happening until she felt herself start to unravel.

"Ryan. Oh, Ryan." Then she made incoherent noises as a million tiny stars burst into life behind her eyelids.

Shockwaves rolled over her, each one smashing her safeguards and leaving her trembling and overwhelmed. It was all too good. Too perfect. Too much. Tears poured down her cheeks and she threw her arm across her eyes to hide them. Surely no man who'd just given a woman such an explosive orgasm would want to see her bawling in the aftermath.

"That was incredible," she told him, the hitch in her voice betraying her emotion.

"I'll say." Ryan eased up her body and trailed kisses along her neck. "I've never known anyone who comes the way you do. I'm going to take you upstairs and get you naked. Then you're going to do that all over again. And again."

Zoe lifted her arm off her face and looked at Ryan. His gray eyes had an earnest glow that made her heart skip a beat.

"Sound good?" he prompted.

She nodded. "Really good."

Laughter and panting bounced off the walls of the wide staircase as they raced to his second-floor master suite. Usually, Ryan would've had the advantage with his longer legs, but they were stripping off their clothes as they ascended and Zoe's dress and bra seemed to fall off her body with very little effort while Ryan fumbled with his clothes.

Then, too, he was slowed by the glorious sight of her nakedness as she crooked her finger and lured him after her. After shedding his shirt and tie, he wrestled off his socks and nearly tripped over his pants. Sucking in a giant breath, he turned the corner and entered his bedroom.

Ryan came to a dead stop at the sight of Zoe standing near the window overlooking the garden. She'd draped herself in the curtain and the challenge on her face told him she expected to be unwrapped in spectacular fashion. Putting on a mock scowl, he stalked toward her.

"You said you wanted to get me naked," she reminded him, clinging to the fabric. "I got you partway there."

Grinning, Ryan plucked the curtain from her grip. "Thank you for that," he said. "But now I want to see all of you."

He took her by the hand and twirled her. Zoe was all lean, hard muscle and athletic curves. Her breasts were small, but the round shape was perfect and he couldn't wait to get his mouth on them again.

"You are gorgeous," he declared, lifting her into his arms and carrying her to his bed.

"So are you," she murmured, her fingers tunneling into his hair.

He followed her onto the mattress, taking her nipple into his mouth and rolling his tongue around the plump tip until it became a hard bud. Zoe's husky moan filled his ears, making him smile as he repeated the move with her other breast. He kept his fingers skimming over her face, her torso, her thighs, wanting to return her to the keen state of arousal that had led to her explosive climax earlier.

He trailed his lips over her shoulder and breasts one last time before reclaiming her mouth in a kiss. Curving his fingers around the back of her head, he drove his mouth against hers, devouring her while encouraging noises erupted from her throat, urging him on.

She spread her legs and slid her hands over his hips, urging him between her thighs. He hooked his fingers behind her knee and lifted it toward his waist, opening her. The move allowed him to settle his erection against her wet heat. He groaned as the pressure drove his lust higher, and then he was grinding against her and she rocked in frenzied movements, moaning and arching her back.

Incoherent thoughts swam through Ryan's head as his mouth fell to her throat and his teeth sought for purchase against her skin. The light nip he gave her caused her hips to buck. He met the move with a deep thrust, letting her incredible wetness soak the fly of his boxers.

"I promised myself I'd take it slow," he growled, warning her that he was more than a little out of control. "But I just can't wait to be inside you."

"I need that, too."

"It's going to be amazing. I promise—"

She sent both hands diving under the waistband of his boxers and dug her nails into his butt muscles just as he thrust into her again. His hips jerked forward, bumping him against her with more force than he intended. To his surprise she matched his fierce charge with a roughness that send an electric surge of pleasure down his spine.

It took him a second to realize she'd tugged his underwear down. But when the fabric hooked on his erection and she began to tug frantically, he came to his senses and eased her hands away before she damaged him beyond saving.

"Wait," he murmured. "I need to get a condom."

"Hurry."

If every atom in his body wasn't focused on what

was to come, he might have smiled at her eagerness. Instead he concentrated all his energy on digging a foil packet out of his nightstand, tearing it open and rolling the condom onto his erection with hands that shook.

While he'd been so occupied, she hadn't been idle. She'd thrown off the comforter and top sheet, leaving nothing on the bed to interfere with their lovemaking. Now, as he stood beside the bed, his shaft pointing directly at her, she reclined on her elbows. Offering him a small, satisfied smile, she parted her legs and let him drink his fill of the lush, rosy perfection that awaited him between her thighs.

With a shaky exhale, Ryan moved over her and rubbed the tip of his erection against her. Her head fell back and she moaned greedily. The glorious sound made him smile. He pushed a little way in and the wet slide into her tight heat made him shudder with pleasure.

"That's it," she moaned, her entire body vibrating as he slid deeper.

Her fingers curved into his back, nails digging. The sharp pain zinged along his already overwhelmed nerve endings as he pulled back and drove forward again.

"Like that?" he asked.

"Perfect." She purred the word, her eyes slipping shut.

"This is just the beginning," he promised her. "Don't hold back."

"Never."

And she didn't. She cried out at every thrust, giving herself over to him. It was a beautiful thing to watch as her earlier wildness became fierce demand. She rode her desire for dear life, claiming her pleasure without reservation. Equal parts awe and pride suffused him at the exquisite focus on her face.

Ryan slid his hand over her hip and drove into her harder. She moaned his name and he tried to form words to convey how he felt about her. What being inside her did to him.

"I need to come with you inside me," she moaned, her husky voice rasping pleasantly against his raw nerve endings. "Make me come, Ryan."

Her command echoed his need. Although he'd already given her one orgasm tonight, sharing a second one with her became his top priority. But already he was closer to finishing than he wanted to be. Being inside her short-circuited his willpower. He was too close to the edge. And he needed her to be there with him.

He shifted his hips and thrust into her at a different angle. She clutched him hard and the noises she'd been making morphed into something eager and frantic. Cracks appeared in the dam holding back his pleasure. He clenched his teeth, unsure how much longer he could keep his release at bay.

The need to connect with her overwhelmed him. He opened his eyes and looked down at her. Lust blasted through him when he realized she was watching him. Their gazes tangled and locked. Something tore loose in Ryan's chest as he realized he was exactly where he wanted to be. Not just buried deep in Zoe. But with her in this moment, watching her slowly shatter beneath him.

An electric, dangerous emotion sizzled down his spine and tightened his gut, then he felt nothing but searing heat and pounding heart and endless desire.

"Come with me, baby," he urged while all the stars in the sky blazed to life in his mind. "Please. Come with me."

But she needed no urging. She moaned his name, shock plain on her features. A shudder racked her torso as her breath came in ragged pants. They tumbled over the edge together and for what seemed like minutes Ryan shook with pleasure as his orgasm shocked his system over and over.

His muscles failed him and Ryan dropped onto his elbows, somehow managing at the last second to spare Zoe the full crush of his weight.

A curse rattled through his unsettled thoughts. What the hell had just happened?

"That was absolutely amazing," she declared unsteadily, her fingers gliding over his shoulder. "You are a wonder."

He was a wonder? Did she have any idea what she had just done to him?

Ryan rolled them across the mattress until she lay sprawled in languorous repose atop his chest. Tangling his fingers in her hair, he tugged until she met his gaze. The contact was brief and unsatisfying.

"You're magnificent."

Even as he spoke, the description struck him as less than satisfactory after what had just happened between them, and he was surprised when she winced away from the compliment.

"I've never known…" She trailed off without finishing her thought. "I didn't know."

"Didn't know what?"

Her fingertips created swirls on his sweat-dampened shoulders. He watched her face, trying to read her expression and guess at her thoughts. It turned out he didn't yet know her as well as he hoped because he had no idea what was behind her pensiveness.

"Until now I've only ever been with one man."

That one man being her husband. Ryan didn't respond and shifted his gaze to the ceiling, giving her space to share and work through what was on her mind.

"I suppose in this day and age that seems very backward," she continued in a rueful tone.

Once again she was making assumptions about his opinions. Why did she always believe that her choices were the wrong ones?

"Not necessarily." Ryan dusted his fingers down her spine. "You were young when you got married."

"Not that young. I was twenty. Lots of girls have sex in high school."

"Not everyone is ready to take that step so early."

"I don't know if I was or wasn't. Boys didn't notice me. I was too quiet. Utterly forgettable."

"Now *that* I don't believe."

If he'd met her at seventeen would he have been equally blind? Probably. Only a mature man could appreciate a woman with complex layers. Had that been the case with her ex-husband? There had been a ten-year age gap between them. Yet from everything Zoe had—

and hadn't—said about her ex, it didn't sound like the man had wanted to cherish, only to control.

"It's true. I was pretty socially awkward. I still am. As Tristan's wife I learned to handle myself in public, saying all the right things, joining the right groups, making the right friends." Bitterness gave her voice a sharp edge. "I lost sight of who I was."

"I think most people wear some sort of façade in public," he said. "We want to fit in and be liked."

"You don't do that."

His tone was firm as he said, "We all do it."

"Until I met you I'd forgotten how nice it was to speak my mind and not worry about the consequences."

Consequences? Ryan frowned. What sort of cost had she endured just because she'd voice her opinion? His chest tight with emotion, Ryan wrapped his arms around her and buried his face in her neck.

Playing the part of Zoe's hero might lead him down a dangerous road. The last time he'd tried to rescue a damsel in distress it had backfired spectacularly. Yet tonight he'd embarked on a journey. A first step back to trust. And Ryan couldn't bring himself to slow down.

Eight

Zoe caught herself humming as she worked on the books in her "office" in the back room of Second Chance Treasures. For the first time since she'd signed the lease, Zoe glimpsed light at the end of the tunnel and knew they were going to be okay. The relief made her feel lighter than air.

Or maybe her positive outlook had more to do with Ryan.

After being married to Tristan for eight years, she was cynical enough to attribute her happy glow to all the fantastic sex she and Ryan were having, but deep down she acknowledged there was more to it. She enjoyed hanging out and talking with Ryan. And the man actually listened while she went on and on about her hopes for the store and the challenges of helping victims of domestic abuse. He didn't shy away from her need to vent and Zoe valued that as much as she did his glorious kisses.

"Here's the mail," Jessica said, setting a stack of envelopes on the desk and startling Zoe out of her musing. "Is it okay if I head to lunch in ten minutes?"

"Sure." She realized it was nearly noon. She saved the spreadsheet she'd been working on and closed her laptop. "I'll just go through the mail real quick, and then come up front."

"No hurry. The morning rush has mostly cleared out and Eva mastered the register really fast."

With the store's desperate and immediate financial pressures eased somewhat, Zoe had hired Eva to replace Magnolia. Like Jessica, Eva had a school-age child, a daughter with her mother's blond hair and big brown eyes. She had a neighbor who could watch the little girl on Saturdays so Eva could pick up some extra hours at the store.

In the wake of the theft, Zoe had pondered what to do about reporting the stolen money. After much soul searching, she'd chosen not to pursue legal action. Magnolia had never struck her as a thief. If she needed the money that badly, her situation must have been desperate. And Zoe was all too familiar with how that felt.

Besides, the way traffic continued to increase over the last couple of weeks, the store was in a much better situation. She might be able to bring on even more help. The irony wasn't lost on Zoe. None of this would be possible without Ryan and Susannah's support. Zoe had wormed her way into the candidate's orbit so she could dig up dirt. Instead she'd been helped by Susannah working her connections to bring Second Chance Treasures to the attention of other well-meaning socialites. The word-of-mouth advertising had brought women in, but it was the quality of the inventory that encouraged them to pull out their wallets.

It seemed as if ever since she'd set foot in Susannah's campaign headquarters, her financial and emotional situations had taken a positive turn thanks to the Dailey siblings. And how was she responding to their kindness? With betrayal and lies.

Hundreds of times a day she sought a way out of her pledge to harm Susannah, knowing that Everly wouldn't listen to any of Zoe's pleas to escape their revenge bargain. Everly was determined to have her pound of flesh and expected Zoe to serve it up on a silver platter.

Plagued by gut-churning anxiety, Zoe made quick work of sorting the mail. Most of it was advertising and catalogs. She set the phone bill on the pile of invoices she needed to write checks for and reached for the final envelope. It was large and plain with only her name and the store's address neatly printed on the front. Expecting it was one of those tricks companies used to pique someone's curiosity so they'll open the envelope instead of sending it straight to the trash, Zoe slit it open and pulled out the contents.

At first she had trouble registering what she held. Quickly, however, uneasiness spread through her as she realized it was pages and pages of legal documents and bank statements belonging to a series of limited liability companies. There were five companies in all, each owned by a different LLC entity. The exact meaning of what she was staring at escaped her, until she scanned the paperwork for the last company and noted her ex-husband's name.

An electric shock blasted through her. She matched up the legal documents with the bank statements. Here was the money Tristan had hidden from her. He'd created a series of foreign shell companies to conceal his funds, but the banks he'd used were all located in the United States. How could he do something like that and get away with it?

That was a question for someone knowledgeable in such matters. Zoe considered if she should take this to her divorce lawyer. The idea of going up against Tristan in court a second time with Sherman Sutter at her side gave her pause. He'd been badly outmatched by Tristan's team of sharks. It almost wasn't fair to put him through what would likely be an even more contentious fight.

The bell on the store's front door tinkled merrily, reminding Zoe that Eva was alone out front. She tucked the papers back in their envelope and slid them into the desk drawer. Then, feeling as if she'd just been handed a ticking time bomb, Zoe headed into the store.

Not even a steady stream of customers could keep Zoe's thoughts off the implications of the documents in her possession. Once the shock had worn off, it had occurred to her that they'd probably come from London. How she'd managed such a daring feat, Zoe had no idea, but it drove home a painful truth.

Everly and London had completed their part of the

bargain. Now it was up to Zoe to either find or fabricate something that would damage Susannah's campaign. The thought of hurting Ryan or his sister made her ill, but she couldn't back out of the plan. Everly was too invested in avenging her sister to ever let Zoe walk away.

Ryan flopped onto his back, chest heaving. On the living room rug beside him, Zoe was equally winded. As they panted in unison, he found that he was grinning. Once again they'd been unable to make it upstairs to his bedroom. They hadn't even managed to get fully undressed before lust had overpowered them.

Since finding out Zoe was on birth control and they'd agreed condoms weren't necessary, every room on the first floor had seen some sort of action. Ryan couldn't seem to keep his hands off her and Zoe had proved an eager and willing partner.

"Damn," he murmured in appreciation. "We did it again."

"Third time this week," Zoe agreed, sounding somewhat bemused. "I've never been like this before."

Ryan turned his head and gazed at her profile. "Like what?"

"Horny all the time." She heaved a long-suffering sigh. "It's really distracting. And annoying. I'm half as productive as I used to be."

"I like this new side of you." In fact, he liked all sides of her.

Without moving her head, she shifted her gaze from the ceiling to him. "What new side of me?"

"The one where you're a lot more open."

"How do you figure I'm more open?"

"When we first met you were a closed book. Now you speak your mind."

"It's not always polite to do so."

"Maybe not," Ryan said, "but it's real." He ran his lips across her shoulder, sending a shiver down her arms. "I can work with real."

"What does that mean?"

Zoe sat up and started to pull her clothes back into place, signaling the end of their intimacy. She was often skittish after they made love, as if she regretted letting go. Her defensive behavior left Ryan wondering what had gone on during her marriage. So far he hadn't pried, but his curiosity was getting the best of him.

He'd already concluded that she was a survivor. Not that she'd confided any such thing, but her passionate stand against domestic violence hinted that she'd been a victim herself.

"I hope you realize that this has grown past a casual fling for me," Ryan said, deciding to put his cards on the table in a show of good faith. "I want you to be able to trust me."

"I do."

Her quick answer didn't satisfy him. "Sometimes I feel like I barely scratch the surface with you."

She drew her knees to her chest and faced him. "I've spent a lot of years hiding my true feelings."

"You don't have to do that with me."

"Opening up scares me." She set her chin on her knees and avoided his gaze. "I feel vulnerable and exposed."

"What do you expect me to say or do to hurt you?"

"Nothing." Yet her flat expression and closed body language said otherwise. "I don't think you're the sort of person who would judge or ridicule me."

Meaning others had come before him who had. "Did your ex-husband do those things?"

"I don't want to rehash my marriage."

"I'll take that as a yes."

She scowled. "You are so annoying."

"So you've mentioned." He grinned at her, preferring insults to carefully worded statements that hid her true emotions. "You know I'll eventually get the truth out of you, so why not just come clean now?"

"Ugh." Zoe pushed to her feet and stalked to the dining table where they'd abandoned plates of chocolate cake to feast on each other. She returned with one of the decadent desserts and plopped down beside him. "Why would you want me to talk about my relationship with Tristan?"

"Because I want to know more about you and I think you're holding on to a lot of pain and anxiety about your marriage."

She popped a bite of cake into her mouth and took her time savoring the flavors. "He was very controlling and highly critical of my appearance." As she spoke, she offered him a forkful of cake.

"You're a stunningly beautiful woman," he told her, his tongue flicking out to catch a bit of chocolate off his lip. "What is there to be critical of?"

"He wanted me to look a certain way. I was expected to be thin, but without muscle definition. He demanded my hair be a certain length and color. He preferred me in pastels, pink, peach or blues, and hated any shades of yellow or green. No bright colors and no black." Her hand shook as she speared into the cake once more. "I learned early on not to voice my opinion or to offer suggestions."

"Why did you marry him?" The question came out more bluntly than Ryan would've wished, but he couldn't reconcile the Zoe he'd come to know with the woman she was describing and needed to understand.

"I was young and naïve and I didn't have a clear sense of what I wanted to do with my life. My mother was thrilled that I'd caught the interest of a handsome, wealthy businessman and pushed me to 'be smart' every time I doubted if he was the right man for me." While she talked, Zoe devoured the rest of the cake as if the sugary dessert eased her discomfort.

"So your new look…" Ryan indicated her short hair and the long graphic tank she wore like a minidress that bared the strong, sexy muscles in her arms and legs. Her over-the-knee boots lay a little distance off. "Is it a complete rejection of everything your ex demanded or the real you?"

A fleeting smile crossed Zoe's lips. "There's no question I'm rebelling. When I first cut my hair, I felt empowered and revolutionary."

"Now?"

She shrugged. "I'm a work in progress." Her gaze caught his. "Does that bother you?"

"Why should it?" He had no intention of judging her. "I like to think we're all evolving."

"Even you?"

He'd asked her to talk about herself, so it was only fair that he share a bit of his own inner struggles. "After what happened with Kelly Briggs, I've had a hard time trusting people I don't know well."

"Like me?"

"Yes." He wondered if he should come clean about his ongoing suspicions. If he kept silent and the truth came out later, it might damage their intimacy during a period when their relationship was heating up. "When you first volunteered for Susannah's campaign, we all thought you were working for Abernathy."

"And now you believe otherwise."

Ryan paused a beat before answering. "The reason I caught your lease up was because your landlord is a friend of Abernathy's and I wondered if they were using your financial problems as a way to get you to spy."

Zoe's eyes widened. "But that was only little over a week ago. You still thought I might be working for Abernathy when we…" She shook her head. "And now?"

"Now, I—"

"Wait," she said, interrupting him. "I understand if you still don't trust me. I haven't exactly been an open book. And after what happened with your company, you have every reason to be suspicious."

Taking the empty plate from her, Ryan set it aside and slid his fingers around the back of her neck, drawing her in for a kiss. "But I don't want to be," he told her, his lips drifting against hers. "I think there's something really great happening between us and I don't want our past experiences to mess up what's going on now or what could develop in the future."

As he finished speaking he noticed how Zoe's muscles had gone still. He glanced down at her expression and noticed her frown. Was he moving too fast? She'd only recently finalized her bitter, contentious divorce. Maybe she wasn't ready to think about a future with him.

Just as Ryan was wondering whether he should walk back his declaration, Zoe scooted closer and put her hand on his knee and said, "That's exactly how I feel."

As she pushed her lips hard against his, stirring the explosive chemistry between them to life once more, hazy suspicion lingered in the wake of her declaration. However, before he could pursue the questions that infiltrated his thoughts, they were incinerated by a fiery rush of passion.

On the Saturday of Susannah's fund-raiser, Zoe regarded her reflection while a familiar anxiety created a lump in her stomach. As she'd applied her smoky makeup and slipped into the strapless navy gown embellished with gold sequins, she'd been imagining the shocked disapproval of her former acquaintances as they took in her short blond hair and celestial-themed dress.

One purpose in changing her look had been to reinvent herself postdivorce. But had she gone too far?

It frustrated Zoe that she cared what anyone from her previous life thought. Maybe the resilience she'd gained in the wake of her divorce was proving to be more fragile than she'd hoped.

Had it been a mistake to attend an event where she ran the risk of crossing paths with people from her past? Only time would tell. At least she wouldn't have to face them alone. She'd be on Ryan's arm and that was a huge confidence booster.

A knock sounded on her front door, jolting her out of her reverie. Mouth dry, palms clammy, she rushed to it, hoping to see Ryan's eyes light up when he saw her. Swinging the door open, she stared at the man standing before her. His broad shoulders looked even more imposing clad in a flawlessly tailored tuxedo jacket. Instead of the traditional black bow tie, he'd chosen to accent his crisp white shirt with a dark gray tie dotted with white. She loved his unconventional approach to formal wear.

"Wow," she murmured, leaning against the door while she took him in. "You look great."

His slow smile sent heat rushing through her. "You look pretty wonderful yourself. Let me get a better look at you." He captured her hand and spun her slowly. "Gorgeous."

The approval glowing in his gray eyes unraveled the knot of worry in her chest. If she'd believed herself past the point where she required a man's praise, she'd been completely wrong. But Ryan was different in that he would have appreciated anything she'd chosen to wear. Not once had he passed judgment on her appearance.

When she'd left Tristan's house, she'd abandoned most of her formal wardrobe, except this one dress that she'd bought, knowing Tristan would never let her wear it. The mermaid-style gown showed off her toned arms and clung to her lean curves, accentuating her sensuality. In it she felt sophisticated and strong, two things she'd never known during the years she'd been married to Tristan.

"I'm going to be the luckiest guy there tonight with you as my date."

"And I'm the luckiest girl," she murmured, for the moment letting herself bask in the glow of his admiration.

For several heartbeats they stood grinning at each other and then Ryan tugged at her hand. "Let's get going. The sooner we put in an appearance, the quicker I can get you home and out of that dress."

"And here I thought you liked it," Zoe teased, pulling the door shut behind her.

"I love it." He wrapped his arm around her waist and bent his lips to her ear. "It's just that I love your beautiful soft skin so much more."

She felt goose bumps at his words. He had a knack for turning her on with a look or a compliment. She became aware of the pulse throbbing between her thighs as she anticipated his hands coasting over her body, stripping the gown away, baring her to his gaze and touch. A groan built in her chest as desire bloomed, but she held it in and savored the rush of longing that flowed through her veins.

Being around Ryan made her happier than anything she'd known before. On the heels of this realization came a bitter reality check. The purpose behind why she'd met him in the first place. The reason she'd moved into his spare apartment and had cultivated his friendship was to cause him harm.

Despair struck at her, ruining her mood. Her smile faded as they neared Ryan's car. He noticed the sudden change and pulled her into his arms before opening the car door.

His thumb caressed her cheek. "What's wrong?"

"Nothing." The lie came easily to her lips. So did the reassuring smile.

She'd spent most of her married life pretending to be something she wasn't. Lately she'd felt safe enough to display her true emotions. Ryan was a rock that she could batter with sarcasm, anger and tears. Nothing she said or did seemed to faze him. He absorbed everything and gave back understanding and acceptance.

"Are you worried about seeing your ex?"

"It's not just him. Everyone I used to know will be there tonight. They're all going to be judging me." Perhaps it wasn't the whole truth, but it was true enough to justify her sudden bout of melancholy.

"You don't have to let their opinions matter," he reminded her. "They can't hurt you unless you let them."

"You're right." She heaved a sigh. "It's just really hard to stop caring that they disapprove."

The admission wasn't one she'd confided to anyone before Ryan. She trusted him not to dismiss her concerns. Somehow he recognized how determined she was to face up to the challenges she'd once avoided.

"You'll get there." He kissed the top of her head. "In the meantime, you can count on me to play guard dog for you. I'll bare my teeth at anyone who makes you uncomfortable."

She smiled as no doubt he'd hoped she would. Grinning at him released more of her tension. She captured his face between her palms and kissed him firmly on the lips.

"Thank you," she said, feeling her heart expanding as she gazed at him.

"I'm serious."

"I know." She released him and stepped back. "And you're a wonderful champion." *I don't deserve you.*

The thought continued to ring in her mind as Ryan drove them to the venue, and even when he tucked her hand into the crook of his arm and led the way into the party. Her agitation grew with each stride into the historic downtown Charleston plantation home overlooking the Ashley River. Who would she run into at tonight's thousand-dollar-a-plate fund-raiser for Susannah's state senate campaign?

"Zoe Crosby." A beautiful brunette stepped into her path. "I almost didn't recognize you. You cut all your hair off." Before Zoe could update Polly Matson with her post-divorce surname, the woman's keen blue eyes shifted in Ryan's direction and lingered. "Obviously divorce agrees with you." She stuck out a slender hand tipped with blush-tinted fingernails. "You're Susannah's brother, aren't you? I'm Polly Matson."

"Ryan Dailey." He shook her hand and gave her a polite smile.

"Susannah's brother. You must be so proud of her," Polly gushed, her entire focus coming to bear on Ryan.

"Of course." Ryan nodded. "If you'll excuse us, we were on our way to find her."

"Don't let me hold you up," Polly said as Ryan guided Zoe away.

Zoe didn't need to look back to know that Polly would make a beeline for Callie Hill and Azalea Stocks. The trio had never been all that fond of Zoe before her divorce. No doubt they'd been gleeful when the rumor of Zoe's supposed infidelity had begun to spread. Charleston's elite loved a juicy scandal and of course everyone had come down on Tristan's side. He'd been the model husband, after all. The darker elements of his controlling nature had never made a public appearance. And those pesky rumors surrounding his supposed infidelity? No one cared. Yet Zoe had been shunned after the same allegations had been lodged against her.

"I take it she's not a friend of yours," Ryan said.

"I didn't really have any friends." That sounded overly dramatic so she quickly clarified, "Not true friends anyway. Not the sort you can trust with your darkest secrets and deepest fears."

"Did you have a lot of those? Secrets and fears, I mean."

"Doesn't everyone?"

For several seconds Ryan regarded her somberly. She knew he hated it when she deflected his attempts to understand her better, but she'd spent so long guarding her true feelings that it was second nature to hide behind flippant remarks and bravado.

Zoe gave a huge sigh. "I'm sorry. It's been a while since I felt this exposed."

"I understand."

And she knew he did. He'd proved to be more sensitive to nuance than any man she'd ever known. Was it because his twin was female? Whatever the cause, he knew how to listen.

"Shall we go find Susannah?" she suggested, taking his arm.

The steely muscles beneath the elegant tuxedo jacket reminded her that he'd promised to be her champion tonight and she relaxed slightly. Unfortunately her calm lasted for only a few steps because across the room she spied her ex-husband.

Tristan was deep in conversation with a slender brunette. Although she wanted to tear her attention away, something about the woman struck a chord. The elusive familiarity nagged at her while Ryan paused to chat with a friend. It wasn't until the woman glanced over her shoulder and made direct eye contact that Zoe realized that the brunette was Everly in disguise.

What the hell?

Her anxiety spiked into the red zone as she was swamped by a barrage of questions. What was Everly doing at Susannah's fund-raiser? Why was Everly talking to Tristan? What could possibly be going on? Panic roared through Zoe as she noted their ease with each other. Not once had Everly indicated she'd known Tristan. Was their association a recent development? If so, had she sought him out? Zoe wouldn't put it past her. Damn the woman for stepping over the line again.

Zoe couldn't tear her attention from the pair and when she saw them part ways, she excused herself from

Ryan and headed after Everly. With the other woman demonstrating she had no intention of sticking to their original agreement of no interference, Zoe decided that gave her grounds to back out of the revenge bargain. And it wasn't as if she'd done anything with the documents London had given her about Tristan's financial dealings. If Zoe never went after her ex-husband's offshore accounts technically she'd never get her revenge on him.

Hope bloomed. Maybe there was a way she and Ryan could be together. But first, she intended to get some answers.

She caught up to Everly near the bar and nudged her away from the guests and toward a quiet corner on the far side of the party. Once isolated, she let her irritation show. "What the hell are you doing here and what were you and Tristan talking about?"

"I was just saying hello."

"You were saying hello?" Zoe echoed in disbelief, dumbstruck that Everly could be so flippant about approaching Tristan. "I don't believe you."

"Fine," Everly said, all glibness leaving her manner. "I came to remind you to keep your eye on the ball."

"What's that supposed to mean?"

"It means you've forgotten why you were supposed to get to know Ryan in the first place. We had a bargain, you, London and I. We did our part. Now it's your turn."

"I don't need you riding me all the time. And now I see you talking to Tristan. That's taking things too far." Zoe's hands shook and she gripped her evening bag to keep her anxiety from showing. "In fact, this whole thing is making me uncomfortable." Suddenly Zoe saw a light at the end of the tunnel. A way out of this mess. "I'm done."

Her giddy sense of relief lasted barely a second.

"Excuse me?" Everly's lips tightened and when she spoke next, her words were barely audible. "You can't just quit."

"I can and I am." Zoe's stomach gave a sharp lurch as fury exploded in Everly's bright green eyes. "Because here's the issue. I don't trust you."

With the dinner portion of Susannah's fund-raiser over, Ryan had no interest in lingering. While three of his sister's friends were asking Zoe questions about her store, Ryan went in search of his twin to say goodbye. Seeing that she was deep in conversation with one of her biggest donors, he decided not to interrupt and was about to reverse direction and head back to Zoe when a man spoke from behind him.

"You really should watch yourself with Zoe."

Ryan turned to confront Tristan Crosby, anger lancing through him at the man's warning. "I don't think that's any of your business."

"She's going to cause you nothing but trouble," Crosby continued smoothly, as if Ryan hadn't spoken.

"Seems to me you're the one looking to create problems," Ryan responded, his tone hard and cold. "Why don't you mind your own business and let Zoe get on with her life?"

"You know, my ex-wife is full of sob stories," Tristan

said, undaunted by Ryan's warning. "The last thing you want to do is believe everything she says."

Although he regretted engaging the man, Ryan had promised to defend Zoe. "I have no reason to doubt anything she says." Yet at one point in time hadn't he done exactly that? Of course, that was before they'd started sleeping together.

The explosive chemistry Ryan enjoyed with Zoe had blunted his initial reservations about her.

As if Zoe's ex could read Ryan's mind, a cruel smirk formed on his lips. "She's good at keeping secrets, but I think you'll find that out soon enough."

When Ryan refused to respond, Crosby offered a mocking salute before walking away. The exchange had been both brief and unpleasant, yet its disturbing aftertaste lingered in Ryan's mind. Obviously, Crosby wasn't satisfied with all the damage he'd done to Zoe during the divorce proceedings. He intended to pursue his grudge even further.

"Why were you talking to Tristan?" Zoe demanded as she approached him, her frightened expression startling Ryan.

"He was just trying to cause trouble between us."

Zoe frowned. "What did he say?"

Ryan cursed the distrust Tristan Crosby had stirred in him. Thanks to all the fantastic sex Ryan had been having with Zoe, he'd stopped suspecting her.

"He made some vague warnings about you being trouble," Ryan replied, his tone dismissive. At the horror reflected in her expression, he added, "I set him straight, and then told him to back off and leave you alone."

"Thank you for standing up for me." She reached out and took his hand in a fierce grip. "It's not something I'm use to."

Her appreciation left him feeling guilty for his earlier doubts. Suddenly he was remembering what had happened with Kelly Briggs. When he'd discovered her boyfriend had locked her out of the apartment they'd been sharing and wouldn't give her back her stuff, Ryan had found her a new place to live and persuaded the ex to turn over her things as well as to give up several expensive items Kelly had purchased while they'd been living together.

While Ryan had never crossed a line with Kelly because she'd been his employee and he hadn't been attracted to her in the least, he missed how emotionally vulnerable she was. To his dismay, she'd misinterpreted his motivation behind aiding her and created a fantasy where he'd felt something for her beyond friendship. When he'd set her straight, she'd overreacted to his rejection and retaliated by deleting his company's important engineering schematics.

Ryan recognized that he'd made a huge mistake with Kelly Briggs. Had he repeated the error with Zoe? Would his actions once again come back to bite him in the ass?

His choice to invite her to stay in one of his guest apartments had been far from prudent, but lust had proved stronger than curiosity or suspicion. He might have overpowered his desire to take her to bed if their chemistry had been less explosive.

The speed with which things had been moving between them coupled with Crosby's warning awakened Ryan to just how fast Zoe had slid beneath his skin. Should he tap on the brakes? Her financial situation wasn't the best. Did his wealth make him more attractive to her? She hadn't asked him for help, yet she'd made it clear that her situation was desperate.

Ryan believed he'd resolved the questions surrounding Zoe joining Susannah's campaign. He'd been lulled by their deepening connection to invite her into his inner circle. Now, Crosby's ambiguous threats reminded Ryan that in many ways she remained an unknown entity. If things fell apart with their fledgling relationship, would she act out the way Kelly had? What sort of fallout should he brace for?

Her fingers tightened around his. "What are you thinking about?" she asked, peering at him in concern and leaving him to wonder if his expression had revealed his inner turmoil.

"Let's get out of here," he said, pushing aside his doubts about what was or wasn't real about their relationship. "I think I've supported my sister long enough."

"Sure." The smile she gave him would've appeared perfectly natural if it had reached her eyes. "I'm dying to be alone with you."

Her response was perfect. Too perfect? Disgusted with himself, Ryan led her toward the exit. "Do you want to grab a drink somewhere or head straight home?"

"Let's go back to your place," she said, leaning into him. "I want to get naked with you."

Her whispered words sent lust raging through him, but Ryan couldn't stop himself from wondering if she was saying what she knew he wanted to hear or if sex was truly on her mind. It would be so easy to take her at face value. He could just consider himself incredibly lucky to be involved with a woman whose passion matched his own.

"Keep talking like that and I'll get pulled over for speeding," he teased, shoving aside his doubts for the rest of the evening.

Everly sat in her car outside Susannah Dailey-Kirby's campaign headquarters, replaying her latest conversation with Devon Connor and wondering how long her business would survive if she lost her biggest client. The golf resort magnate was far from happy at her latest ideas to brand the new property he'd purchased and had given her a week to come up with a fresh concept.

Which was why she should be brainstorming at her office instead of watching the campaign staff file out one by one until only the deputy campaign manager remained. In the past, when Everly cruised by at this time of night, she'd noticed Patty Joyce working late, putting in ridiculous hours to make sure everything ran smoothly.

Everly expelled a frustrated breath. Sitting here while nothing was happening was a huge waste of time, but since Zoe had decided to renege on her part of the bargain, it wasn't like Everly had any choice. From the start it was obvious that Zoe lacked commitment. Everly's fury with the former socialite had grown in the days following the fund-raiser and she'd added Zoe to her growing to-do list. As soon as Everly dealt Susannah's campaign a death blow, she would make Zoe pay for turning her back on all Everly's careful planning.

Deciding tonight's surveillance was a bust, Everly took a hold of the keys in her ignition, but before she could fire the engine, she spied a man approaching Joyce. The late hour and darkened storefronts he passed prevented her from seeing his features, but she assumed it was Gil Moore, the campaign manager. Nothing new there. Moore worked as hard as his deputy.

Only as she watched the man approach Patty Joyce, Everly realized she'd guessed wrong. Crowing with delight, Everly lifted her cell phone and zoomed in on Jefferson Kirby as he pulled his wife's deputy campaign manager into his arms and kissed her.

In seconds Everly had captured a dozen images of the couple's passionate embrace. While she waited for them to leave, Everly studied the fuzzy pictures, wishing the faces were clearer. From their body language this wasn't a first-time event.

Moments later the lights went dark and Everly tracked the pair as they headed for Patty Joyce's car. Disappointed that she hadn't done a better job documenting Jefferson Kirby's infidelity, Everly started her car and put it in gear, following the couple.

Their destination turned out to be a motel a mere ten-minute drive from the campaign office with access to the room off the parking lot. With no hallway to walk, they ran less of a chance of being seen. Only, they hadn't counted on Everly.

Thanks to the couple's preoccupation with each other, neither one noticed as Everly parked close enough to capture the whole sordid scene as they kissed their way to the door. The entire spectacle lasted less than thirty seconds, but Everly recorded every instant.

She'd been hoping for dirt on Susannah Dailey-Kirby but, like her brother, the candidate had proved squeaky-clean. Never had Everly expected anything like Jefferson Kirby's affair to fall into her lap, but now that it had, she needed to figure out the best way to capitalize on what she'd uncovered.

Nine

Zoe was picking up lunch for Eva and Jessica at the coffee shop down the street when her phone chimed, indicating an incoming email. With two people ahead of her in line, she'd been scrolling through her social media feed liking cute pictures of cats and sharing photos of the store's newest inventory. The number of people who followed Second Chance Treasures on social media had tripled in the weeks since Susannah had thrown her support behind the store and Zoe was humbled and grateful. If not for Ryan and his sister, Zoe would've had to close the boutique. She owed them an incredible debt.

With so many things going her way, Zoe should've been floating, but she couldn't stop looking over her shoulder at odd moments, expecting to see Everly lurking around every corner. That the other woman hadn't been in contact brought Zoe no peace. Everly's fanatic determination to get revenge on Ryan wasn't going to just vanish because Zoe was no longer participating in the plot and it troubled her that she might now be a target of Everly's vindictiveness.

Zoe glanced at the email that had popped into her inbox, noting the unfamiliar address before the subject line snagged her attention. She read the single word several times while her heart rate skyrocketed.

Busted.

What did that mean? Apprehension surged through her. The only way for her to know for sure was to open the email.

A video file waited below the message Watch this—E. What could Everly possibly be up to now? Bracing herself, Zoe clicked on the attachment and watched in horror as Jefferson Kirby entered a hotel room with his wife's deputy campaign manager, Patty Joyce.

This was the exact sort of dirt that could take down a campaign. Worse, it could destroy two marriages and ruin the lives of both families. The pain that would be unleashed on innocents if this got out would last for years, maybe decades, to come.

She'd volunteered in the hope of finding something exactly this scandalous. That Everly had been the one to uncover the affair instead was unsurprising. The other woman's interference was out of control.

At the end of the short video, Zoe placed her hands against her roiling stomach, contemplating the devastation if this got out. Susannah's campaign might survive the blow, but what about the couple's children? They didn't deserve to be harmed by the vicious gossip the revelation would stir.

Zoe's finger hovered over the delete button. She wouldn't have wished such a difficult situation on her worst enemy, much less someone she admired. But although she longed to erase the email and forget she'd ever seen the video, that wouldn't stop Everly from using it to hurt Susannah. All Everly had to do was to leak the recording to the media or to Lyle Abernathy. He'd make hay with it, gleefully twisting the knife deep into Susannah's heart. He wouldn't care that her husband's affair had nothing to do with the issues or Susannah's ability to represent the people of her district. Instead he would make sure no one could focus on the fact that Susannah was the better candidate.

A familiar rush of helplessness swept over Zoe followed closely by sharp regret. She never should've fallen in with Everly and London. The mad scheme they'd concocted had reached far beyond anything Zoe had imagined and the results hadn't brought her the satisfaction or the peace of mind she'd anticipated. Quite the opposite. Relentless waves of guilt and remorse had torn at her, disturbing her sleep and ruining her appetite. She grappled with how to disengage herself from the revenge bargain and rid herself of Everly. Today's email demonstrated how impossible that would be.

Fifteen minutes later Zoe exited the coffee shop with the lunch order and retraced her steps to the store. With her thoughts racing, she didn't register the tall man approaching her until he spoke.

"Zoe Alston?"

Her attention snapped back to her surroundings and she sized up the bald man in his ill-fitting suit. Was this another of Everly's tricks or the abusive spouse of one of her artisans?

"Can I help you?"

"This is for you." He extended an envelope.

Zoe took it automatically and the man walked away without another word. Besieged by dread, she entered the store and set the lunches on the counter.

"Bianca brought these by a little while ago. Aren't they incredible?" Jessica indicated a stack of watercolor paintings she was recording in the computer. Then, she caught sight of Zoe's face. "Is everything okay?"

"I don't know. A man just handed me this envelope." Zoe held it up, noting the lack of identifying marks. "This just feels wrong."

"You won't know until you open it," Jessica said, displaying the pragmatic nature that had prompted Zoe to hire her.

With a nod, Zoe tore open the flap and pulled out a letter. Anxiety shifted to sorrow as she scanned the lawyer's name before skimming to the meat of the message.

"Looks like the building has been sold and we have thirty days to vacate." Zoe was surprised she managed to maintain a calm tone when everything inside her howled in protest.

"That's terrible. Who would do something like this?"

Zoe reread the letter, paying closer attention to the

details. This time the new owner's name jumped out at her. TA Charleston Holdings, LLC. "TA" as in Tristan Anthony? Zoe reached into her purse for the financial documents belonging to Tristan's shell companies. She'd spent several hours studying the legal paperwork in an effort to make sense of what he'd been up to. She pulled out the sheet containing her notes. There, halfway down the list of names was the one the letter referenced.

Tristan had bought the building containing her store with the sole purpose of kicking her out.

The floor shifted beneath Zoe's feet as the implication struck her and she braced her hand on the counter to steady herself. "Damn it."

She'd foolishly thought there was nothing left for him to take away. Her money was gone. As was her position in the community. Now she was going to lose her store.

"Zoe? Are you okay?"

"It's my ex." She brandished the letter. "He's the one behind this."

Jessica knew all about Zoe's nasty divorce and came around the counter to give Zoe a hug. "We'll get through this," she whispered. "It's going to be okay."

Although Zoe nodded, in her mind she had already started to pack up her inventory. She didn't have the money or the strength to start over a second time.

"I need to clear my head," Zoe said, offering up a wan smile. "Can you and Eva handle things for a little while?"

"We've got this," Jessica said. "Don't worry about anything."

Unsure where she was going, Zoe headed out the

back and got into her car. Her initial instinct had been to call Ryan and spill the news, but then she remembered the video she'd received while at the coffee shop and knew she couldn't dump her problems on him with the threat of the video hanging out there.

No, this was something she had to handle herself. When she reached Crosby Automotive, she parked in an empty visitor spot before marching into the lobby. Pretending to be deaf and blind to the receptionist's greeting, Zoe barreled through the lobby and headed down a series of familiar hallways.

Tristan had a large corner office in the back of the building with floor-to-ceiling windows that overlooked a landscaped stretch of grass and trees. As she neared his assistant's desk, she noticed his door was closed. Usually that meant he was in a meeting. For an instant her rash determination faded. What was she doing? Anything she said or did in the next few minutes was guaranteed to blow back in her face. Tristan was a master at deflection. No matter how badly he behaved, in the end he was never at fault.

"You can't go in there," Ginny Anderson cried as Zoe sailed past and grabbed the doorknob to Tristan's office. "He's in a meeting."

Zoe ignored her and opened the door. Tristan was on the phone. His eyes widened when she stepped in and shut the door behind her.

"Someone just came in," he said to whoever was on the other end of the call. "I have to go. I'll call you later." Hanging up, he got to his feet and came around the desk. "What the hell do you think you're doing bursting in on me like that?"

Once his anger would've cowed her, but she was no longer the woman he'd dominated. She stared her ex-husband down as he approached, refusing to back down as he came to tower over her.

"You bought my building so you can evict me?" She brandished the letter. "That's low even for you."

His eyes narrowed. "How'd you know it was me?"

She immediately saw her mistake. Without the documents she'd received about his shell companies she'd have no idea he was behind her eviction. Zoe hiked her purse higher on her shoulder, the weight of Tristan's secrets a burden she should've left in the car.

"Who else could it be?" she retorted, bluffing like her life depended on it. "You've done your best to ruin me. This is just another in a long list of dirty tricks."

"You seem pretty certain it was me," he replied smoothly. "You must have some sort of proof."

His absolute confidence suggested he knew exactly what had been sent to her.

Inwardly cursing that she hadn't thought her accusation through, she said, "I have no idea what you're talking about."

"I know what you've been up to." He leaned into her space, his manner growing even more menacing.

"I haven't been up to anything." Zoe took a firmer grip on her purse.

"You're a liar." Without warning, Tristan whipped his hand forward, latched onto her handbag and yanked it off her shoulder. "Do you have it with you?"

"Stop that!" Zoe snagged the strap and held on. "Let go! What are you doing?"

With a sharp sideways jerk, Tristan stripped the purse from her hands. Pulled off-balance, she stumbled and nearly fell. By the time she straightened, Tristan had freed the envelope. He threw the bag at her feet. Fighting helpless tears, Zoe scooped up her purse and held it against her chest.

"You have no right," she cried, wondering why she thought this encounter would go in her favor when none had before.

"I have every right." He scanned the contents of the envelope, mouth tightening at what he found. "You were stupid to bring this with you today." While Zoe watched in helpless dismay, Tristan tossed the envelope onto his desk and straightened his tie. "But then you've never been all that smart."

Zoe barely registered the insult. Her throat tightened as she fought overwhelming despair. Because of her rashness, she'd lost the only leverage she'd had against him.

"That boyfriend of yours has no idea about you," Tristan continued, more relaxed now that he'd regained the upper hand. "Or what you've been up to."

"What are you talking about?" she demanded, cursing the impulse to engage him.

Her stomach clenched in fear as a sly smile appeared on his face, making it clear he knew every sordid detail of what she'd been doing.

"You know," he said. "The little revenge pact you made where you receive dirt on me in exchange for you getting dirt on Dailey's sister. I had no idea you had it in you."

"How...?"

Only three people knew about that. London would never risk her reputation by telling anyone. And unless she'd started talking in her sleep, Zoe hadn't spilled the beans.

"Your friend Everly told me," Tristan said, confirming Zoe's conclusion.

"Who?" she asked breathlessly, hearing the lie.

"Everly Briggs." Tristan smirked. "I guess she's not as good a friend as you thought."

"She's not my friend. She's barely even an acquaintance." At least that much was true.

"Don't bother denying it," he countered. "She told me you had someone steal information from my computer."

Zoe was sure Everly hadn't sent the documents, so how had she known? "Sounds like a pretty fantastic story."

"It's not a story. It's the truth."

"Like when you accused me of having an affair?" Zoe congratulated herself on her sarcasm. "Those lies didn't work then and they won't work now."

"Really?" He sneered. "How long before Dailey dumps you after he finds out you joined his sister's campaign to gather dirt on her?"

"Stay away from Ryan."

"Or what?"

Yes, or what? Tristan had reclaimed the proof of his illegal activities.

"It's your word against mine," she blustered. "And he already knows better than to trust you."

"Maybe, but he's been burned before," Tristan said, spilling just how thoroughly Everly had betrayed their pact. "I'm going to guess that he's not going to make the same mistake twice. And that means all I have to do is make one little phone call and you two are done."

With grief rising to nearly intolerable levels, Zoe pivoted on her heel and walked out of Tristan's office. Although she'd closed her eyes to the inevitable, she'd known her relationship with Ryan would eventually end in heartbreak.

But she would be damned if either Everly or Tristan dealt the killing blow. If she and Ryan were over, Zoe would be the one to shatter the connection.

Suspecting that Tristan would hold off calling Ryan to torment her as long as possible, Zoe pulled out her phone and dialed Ryan's number.

"Something has come up," she said after he picked up. "We need to talk…"

After Zoe's dire "we need to talk" declaration and her unwillingness to get into anything more over the phone, Ryan spent several minutes wondering if he was facing the abrupt end of their relationship and disturbed at the idea of losing her. Luckily, the rest of his day was taken up by a series of meetings that left him too busy to dwell on what she had on her mind.

Now, however, as he stood in his kitchen, pondering what to do for dinner, Ryan considered how fast he'd gotten used to having Zoe around all the time. They ate together most nights, either at his house or at one of downtown Charleston's numerous restaurants. Those dinners often segued into passionate lovemaking and he'd lost count how many times she'd spent the night. Waking up with her in the morning had become his favorite way to start his days.

When a knock sounded on his back door, his heart gave a joyful leap. Many days had passed since he'd given up claiming that he wasn't emotionally engaged. At first he'd told himself such reactions were a predictable chemical response to someone he lusted after. After all, he'd enjoyed the best sex of his life with her.

But it wasn't only physical for him. He'd made an effort to get to know her. Drawn out her fears. Learned about her dreams for the future. Discovered they shared a passion for helping people and a flaw that kept them from spotting trouble before it was too late. And he'd shared parts of himself with her that only his twin had seen.

He went to answer the door and his mood crashed at the somber expression on her face.

"What's wrong?" he asked as she strode past him.

"Everything's messed up," she replied, dumping her purse on the kitchen counter and heading straight to the cabinet in the living room where he kept his liquor. Setting her cell phone down, she indicated the bottles. "Do you mind?"

"Help yourself."

While she poured a healthy shot of vodka into a crystal tumbler, Ryan surveyed her appearance, noting her paleness and smudged eye makeup. She looked as if she'd been crying. What had happened to upset her between their early morning romp and now?

"Feel like talking about it?" he prompted.

"That's why I came by. I need to tell you some things." She finished her drink and poured a second shot. This time, instead of drinking, she rolled the glass between her palms and watched the liquid swirl. "Things you're not gonna be happy to hear."

Her ominous words rousted the doubts he'd put to rest after his encounter with her ex-husband at Susannah's fund-raiser.

"Okay."

But before that happened, he needed to connect with her. Crossing to where she stood, Ryan plucked the glass from her hands. Before she could protest, he pulled her into his arms and kissed her hard. She immediately melted into his embrace. All the tension fled her muscles as she looped her arms around his neck and pressed her body into his. The kiss grew ravenous as frantic, impassioned noises tore from her throat.

Ryan sent his fingertips diving beneath the hem of her sweater dress, eager for the silky warmth of her skin and the tantalizing heat of her arousal. She groaned and sucked his lower lip into her mouth, setting her teeth against the tender flesh as he slid his finger through the wetness between her thighs.

"Oh, Ryan." She gasped when he freed her mouth so he could trail his tongue down her neck and nip at the sensitive cord in her throat.

"I need to taste you," he growled, stripping her thong down her thighs.

Together they sank to the floor. She lay back and Ryan pushed her dress up. Setting his hands on her knees, he pushed them apart, opening her to him.

The noises she made as he drew his tongue along the most sensitive part of her fanned his lust to white-hot brilliance. He ignored the tight ache below his belt and focused on driving her pleasure higher. By now he knew both a fast and slow way to make her crazy, but she'd learned a thing or two about him, as well.

"I want to come with you inside me," she panted, tugging on his hair as her climax drew close. "Please, Ryan."

He had no reason to deny her request and swiftly stripped out of his clothes. She did the same, yanking the Aztec-patterned dress over her head and shimmying out of the tank she wore beneath it. He took a second to admire her lithe, toned body as she set her hand to the zipper of her favorite boots.

With a slow smile, Ryan shook his head. "Leave them on."

This command gifted him with her first smile of the night. She held out her arms and he moved between her thighs. Her gaze locked on his as he slid inside her.

"I love you," she murmured, so quietly that he thought he'd misheard.

His heart gave his ribs a painful kick. An instant later she squeezed her eyes shut and began rocking her hips in the way she knew he adored. Ryan began to move in response and the raw, frenzied lovemaking that followed left him reeling. They climaxed together, Ryan making sure Zoe came hard before surrendering to his own pleasure.

In the aftermath, he lay beside her on the carpet. Completely wrung out, Ryan rolled his head in her direction. She lay with her forearm flung over her eyes, lips parted as her chest rose and fell, lungs laboring. Her skin wore a sheen of sweat, inviting his touch, but she spoke before he could summon the strength to move.

"I need to tell you something," she announced, her tone grim.

"I'm listening."

"Something bad is going to happen to your sister."

His lethargy vanished as a jolt of adrenaline flooded his muscles. Ryan sat up and grabbed her wrist, pulling her arm away from her face so he could see her expression.

"What sort of something?" He heard the suspicion chilling his voice and wasn't surprised when she shivered.

She sat up and pulled free, rubbing her wrist before she tucked her knees against her chest and wrapped her arms around her legs. Her self-protective pose added to his irritation. She had no reason to be afraid of him.

Sorrow filled her eyes. "Jefferson is having an affair with Patty."

For a second he couldn't process her words. Of all the things Ryan was prepared for her to say, hearing that his brother-in-law was cheating wasn't even on the list.

"Susannah's deputy campaign manager?" Ryan shook his head, unable to wrap his mind around Zoe's story. "I don't believe you."

Jefferson would never cheat on Susannah. He adored her. He loved their life and would never do something like that to their children.

"It's true," she insisted. "And there's proof."

"What sort of proof?" he asked, his skepticism raging.

"There's a video."

Damn it all to hell.

"Of what exactly?" he challenged, hoping like hell that she didn't have the goods. That it was all an ill-conceived lie to stir up trouble. Yet what could she possibly hope to achieve by spinning such a tale?

"It's a video of the two of them going into a hotel room."

In this age of technology, things like that could be doctored. And it sounded exactly like something Lyle Abernathy would be behind. Ryan ground his teeth together.

"Have you seen it?" He couldn't just accept her word. Unless he saw it with his own eyes, he'd never accept that Jeff could betray Susannah.

She nodded.

"How? Where?"

Zoe got to her feet and grabbed her cell. She manipulated the phone for a few seconds and then handed it to him.

The video was shot at night and from a distance, but there was no question it was Jefferson Kirby and Patty Joyce and they were romantically involved. The segment was no longer than twenty seconds, but it was more than enough to damn Jeff's actions. Ryan badly wanted to punch something long before the hotel room door shut behind the couple.

"Did you follow them?" He slashed a glance in Zoe's direction and discovered she'd taken the moments of his distraction to put her clothes back on.

Part of his brain mourned that she'd covered up all her beautiful skin, but he recognized that the last thing he needed right now was to be distracted by her nakedness.

"No," Zoe said, retreating to one of the chairs in his living room. "Someone sent the video to me."

"Someone?" he snapped, frustrated by her vagueness. "You mean Abernathy?"

Overwhelmed by fury at Zoe's betrayal, Ryan kicked himself for all the times he'd let lust override common sense when it came to her. From the first he'd suspected something was off about Zoe, but he'd let his hunger for her lead him to stop questioning her abrupt appearance in Susannah's campaign.

"No." Zoe shook her head. "Not Abernathy. He doesn't have anything to do with this."

Not yet.

The unspoken words hung in his thoughts like a deadly virus. There was no doubt that the video would end up in Abernathy's hands eventually. No matter how many assurances Zoe made, the fact that it existed at all meant it would be leaked.

"Who else knows?"

Her gaze pleaded with him for mercy. "I don't know."

"Help me to understand what's going on," Ryan said. "Why did such a damning video come to you?"

The distant rumble of a truck along King Street a few blocks away was the only sound in the room for a long minute until Zoe heaved a weary sigh.

"Because of something I came here to do," she murmured, forcing Ryan to strain to hear her.

"And what is that exactly?"

She wrapped her arms around her waist. If her slumped posture and forlorn expression was supposed to invoke his sympathy, it wasn't working. His blood turned to ice in his veins as he waited for her to speak.

"To mess up your sister's campaign as a way of getting revenge on you."

Ten

Ryan's expression went cold at her words, but Zoe experienced none of the gut-wrenching panic that used to besiege her whenever she'd done something to upset Tristan. No matter how angry he became at her, Zoe trusted Ryan would fight fair.

"Revenge?" Gravel filled his deep voice. "On me? Why? What did I ever do to you?"

"Nothing. It's not me who wants revenge," she explained. "It's Everly Briggs. Because of what happened to her sister Kelly."

"Why would you get involved? Who is Everly to you?"

Ryan pushed to his feet and retrieved his clothes. After slipping back into his boxer briefs and jeans, he thrust his arms into his white button-down shirt and came to stand over her, hands planted on his narrow hips, irritation pulling his brows together.

Although her chest ached, tears hadn't yet made an appearance. For that she should be grateful. Her story would be much harder to tell if she was blubbering incoherently.

"Earlier this fall I went to a networking event and met two women. Everly Briggs and London McCaffrey. I was near the end of my divorce and feeling bitter and helpless. Out of money, beaten up by Tristan's lawyers, I wasn't in my right mind. We were all in a similar state. London was angry at being dumped by Linc Thurston and Everly was devastated that Kelly was in jail. We were all feeling wronged and helpless and vindictive." She stared at her hands, trying to avoid the outrage blazing in Ryan's gray eyes.

"So you decided to get back at us?" Ryan demanded.

Zoe nodded. "We started talking about how great it would be to make you all pay, but knew anything we did would only come back to bite us."

Ryan's expression reflected horrified amazement. "So what did you do?"

"We decided to each go after one of you. We were strangers at a cocktail party. The idea being that whatever bad thing we made happen, it couldn't be traced back to the one who bore a grudge against you. Everly broke up Linc and his housekeeper for London. London secured some documents from Tristan that proved he has money hidden offshore for me."

"And you were supposed to come after me for

Everly," Ryan said. "Only you didn't. You went after Susannah."

Zoe wanted to remind him that she hadn't actually done anything to harm his sister, but recognized it was pointless to defend herself.

"Everly suggested that since you'd hurt her sister," Zoe said. "I should hurt yours."

Ryan stared at her in silence for so long Zoe wondered if he ever intended to speak. His eyes were chips of gray ice, reflecting his mood, and when he next spoke, his tone chilled her to the bone.

"What are you planning to do with the video?"

Zoe gave her head an emphatic shake. "Nothing. Don't you get it? I didn't shoot this. I couldn't do anything to hurt Susannah or you. I lov—" She bit her lip as Ryan threw up a hand, preventing her from finishing. "No," she cried. "I'm going to say it. I love you and I'm sorry about everything. My involvement in this has been eating me up."

"You love me?" he demanded, voice rising in outrage. "I'm supposed to believe that when this whole time you've been lying to me?"

"Only about why I volunteered for Susannah's campaign. You have to believe me." Zoe put her hand on his arm and flinched when he jerked away. "I've been honest about everything else."

"Honest." He growled the word. "Why tell me any of this? You could've just kept quiet and I'd never have known you were involved."

"Everly told Tristan the truth," Zoe admitted, knowing this was the thing that would sink any chance of saving their relationship. If she'd told him the truth before circumstances forced her hand, she might've been able to make him understand. Instead she'd pledged her loyalty to the wrong cause. "He's threatened to tell you."

Ryan rubbed his hands over his face. "That's what he meant at the fund-raiser."

"I did try to back out," Zoe said, doubting he'd believe her. "After getting to know you and Susannah, I couldn't go through with what we'd planned. But Everly was determined to make you pay and she wouldn't listen to reason."

"Do you know what your scheme is going to do to my sister?" Pain filled his voice. "Forget her campaign for state senate, this video will ruin her marriage. Did you stop for one second to think about the potential damage to her family when you started your little game?"

"I'm sorry," she whispered, recognizing mere words could not atone for her mistakes.

Ryan cursed. "I have to warn Susannah." He took several steps in the direction of the hallway before pausing. Without turning around, he delivered his final words. "You need to be gone before I get back."

Ryan grabbed his keys on the way out the back door and headed for the garage. A volatile mix of emotions raged in him, from fury at his brother-in-law's betrayal to despair over the devastation this would cause his sister. Anything related to Zoe he banished to the furthest reaches of his mind.

I love you.

Damn her.

His chest tightened as her declaration reverberated in his mind. Pain and longing battled for dominance. How was it possible that only an hour earlier he'd been reflecting on the mind-blowing sex he'd been having with her and worried that she might want to end things? Ryan bottled up all emotion related to Zoe. She was a distraction he couldn't afford.

He needed to focus his energy on Susannah and to support her as she learned what her husband had been up to.

Before heading to his sister's campaign headquarters, Ryan sent a copy of the video to Paul. He'd forwarded it to himself from Zoe's phone once he'd finished watching it. Now, as he threw his car into reverse and started backing out of the garage, his phone rang.

"What the hell is up with this video you sent me?" Paul demanded, his ferocity feeding Ryan's own ire. "Has Susannah seen it?"

"Not yet. I'm on my way to tell her about it right now."

Paul swore. "Where did it come from?"

"Zoe showed it to me." Ryan clenched the steering wheel until his fingers cramped, but it wasn't enough to overpower the ache in his chest. "It was taken by Everly Briggs."

"Kelly's sister?" Paul sounded as confused as Ryan had been moments earlier. "Why? What's going on?"

"It's a long story."

Ryan went on to repeat what Zoe had told him, keeping the focus on the facts even when his friend's tone grew sympathetic.

"Oh, hell," Paul said. "Susannah doesn't deserve any of this."

"I know. I just wish there was something we could do to mitigate the fallout, but even if we could somehow keep the video from coming out, I don't think that will stop Everly Briggs from further mischief in the future."

"Legally she hasn't done anything wrong," Paul agreed. "How did you leave things with Zoe?"

Ryan was surprised his friend had to ask. "Obviously we're done. I told her to move out."

"Sure, that makes sense." But his tone indicated otherwise.

"She's been lying to me this whole time," Ryan reminded his friend. "Since the day we met."

"Well, to be fair, you suspected her motives for joining the campaign. Turns out you were right. Just the players were different."

"So that somehow makes it okay?" Ryan fumed.

"Not okay, but what exactly is it she did that was so bad besides not tell you what she'd gotten involved in?" Paul asked. "Granted, she started out conspiring against you, but she didn't take any action. And she brought the video to you before it got leaked."

"I can't believe you're taking her side."

"Look," Paul said soothingly, "I get that you're hurt because she wasn't completely honest with you, but it sounds like she got in over her head. It's pretty obvious that Everly Briggs took advantage of her. And, from the sound of things, London McCaffrey as well. I've seen you two together and it's pretty obvious how you feel about each other. Don't let one mistake ruin what you two could have."

I love you.

"You don't get it…" Further protests lodged in his throat. She loved him? How was that possible when she'd lied to and betrayed him?

The video of Jefferson and Patty Joyce played in his mind. His pain was nothing compared to what Susannah was about to feel.

"Ryan?"

He realized Paul had continued talking. "What?"

"I asked if it was okay if I called Zoe about the documents she got from London McCaffrey."

"Sure. Fine."

If Paul was interested, did that mean something illegal had taken place? Would Ryan be responsible for sending two more women to jail? The thought of Zoe behind bars turned his blood to ice.

"Paul, wait a second," Ryan said. "I don't want anything to happen to these women because of me."

"Not even after they conspired to get revenge on you?"

Ryan ignored his friend's amused tone. "Just go at this as my friend, okay? Not as a former cop and cybersecurity specialist."

"Whatever you say. Call me after you talk to Susannah."

"Will do."

Ten minutes after hanging up with Paul, Ryan parked outside the campaign headquarters and headed in. Over half the desks were full of volunteers and campaign staff, most of whom were on the phone. Ryan made a beeline for Susannah's office, unsurprised to find her talking with Gil.

"I need to talk with my sister in private," Ryan said after exchanging a brief greeting with her campaign manager.

"Sure."

Ryan shut the door after the man departed and then lowered all the blinds to ensure complete privacy. Susannah watched him in silence, her eyebrows raised.

"Well, this is dramatic," she said as he sat across from her. "What's going on?"

"I found out something about Zoe today that proves I was right about her motives for coming to work for the campaign."

Susannah's amused expression faded. "Ryan, I'm sorry. I know how much you care about her."

That his sister's first reaction to his news was concern for him was a poignant reminder of why he loved her so much. His heart ached at the blow he was about to deliver.

"It's bad, SuSu." He pulled out his phone and queued up the video. "She's been working with Everly Briggs to mess up your campaign. Today, she showed me this."

He started the video and handed Susannah his phone. Susannah's expression went from confusion to shock and finally horror as she watched her husband head into a hotel room with her deputy campaign manager.

"Zoe took this?" Susannah's neutral tone was at odds with her shaken appearance.

"No. Everly did. I think we can expect this will be leaked to the press or possibly sent to Abernathy at some point in the near future."

"Can you send this to Gil?" Susannah's hands were shaking as she handed the phone back to Ryan. "He'll want to start strategizing damage control as soon as possible." Before she finished speaking, she got to her feet and pulled her purse out of a drawer. "Tell him if he needs to get hold of me later, I'll be at home discussing the situation with Jefferson."

"Is there anything else you need for me to do?" Ryan asked. "Do you want me to come with you and maybe take the kids out for ice cream so you can have the conversation in private?"

"Thanks for the offer, but Candi will be there," Susannah said, referring to her housekeeper. "I'll get her to take them."

Ryan wasn't fooled by his sister's appearance of calm. She was passionate about fair play and justice, and he knew firsthand the painful penalty she dealt when crossed.

"Don't worry about anything here," he told her, catching Gil's eye and motioning him over. "Gil and I will handle everything."

Eleven

It had taken Zoe less than an hour to pack up and vacate Ryan's guest apartment. He'd installed electronic door locks so she had no keys to drop off. In no time at all she was settled back into her storeroom almost as if staying with Ryan had been a wonderful dream she'd awakened from.

In the aftermath of her tempestuous day, Zoe was too overwhelmed to process all that had happened. Thinking about any of it made her chest tight and sent black dots swimming across her vision. She longed for someone to confide in, but couldn't imagine burdening anyone with her story who wasn't already involved. She couldn't contact London…

And yet, why not?

Everly had shattered their pact by telling Tristan that

Zoe had his legal and financial documents. Maybe she'd also divulged that London had been the person responsible for securing the information. In which case, she needed to be warned.

Zoe looked up the address for London's ExcelEvent company. To her surprise, the office was three blocks away from Second Chance Treasures. Impulsively she dialed the phone number. Since it was nearly eight, she didn't really expect anyone would answer.

"ExcelEvent, London McCaffrey speaking."

For several heartbeats, Zoe was too stunned to speak. She hadn't expected getting hold of London would be this easy and had not planned what to say.

"Hello?" London sounded anxious. "Is anyone there?"

"It's Zoe." The words came out of her in a hoarse whisper.

"Zoe, oh my goodness. You scared me. I thought it was Everly. Are you okay?"

Relief swept through Zoe that she wasn't the only one suffering at Everly's hands. "It's all coming apart. I think we should meet and talk."

"I'm at my office. Can you come by now? I don't think we should be seen together in public."

"I'm at my store. Turns out we're just a few blocks apart." She sounded a little hysterical as she relayed that detail. "I'll be by in ten minutes."

The walk helped calm Zoe down and by the time she arrived at ExcelEvent, she was ready to have a productive conversation.

London had been watching for her because before

Zoe could knock, the door opened and the beautiful blonde gestured her inside. Although the two women hadn't been in contact since the Beautiful Women Taking Charge event, they hugged like old friends.

"I love your new look," London told her as they drew apart. "The cut really shows off your bone structure."

"I needed a change," Zoe murmured, feeling no less intimidated by the successful entrepreneur than she had at their last meeting.

"Come into my office."

While London led the way through the reception area and down a hallway, Zoe couldn't help but absorb the chic, elegant offices of ExcelEvent and find them far superior to the casual, eclectic styling of Second Chance Treasures.

"I think we both have a lot to tell each other," London said as the two women settled onto the sofa in her large office.

"First, let me start by thanking you for getting the legal and banking documents from Tristan."

"I didn't," London admitted. "I couldn't. Harrison got them for me."

"Harrison?" Although she liked her former brother-in-law, they hadn't been close and she couldn't imagine why he'd take such a big risk to help her. "Why? How?"

"I told him the truth. All of it. He knows what you've been through and decided to help you out."

That's where London had it wrong. He'd acted to help London. She knew London and Harrison had been seen out together. Until now she hadn't realized they'd become involved.

"But this means he sided against his brother," Zoe said. "Tristan isn't gonna like that."

Pride glowed in London's eyes. "Harrison doesn't care."

"You're in love with him." Sympathy rushed through her. She knew firsthand how difficult it was to find yourself falling for someone you were working against.

"I'm crazy about him."

"How does he feel about you?"

"The same."

Envy speared Zoe straight through the heart. She wanted to be happy like London, forgiven, loved, eagerly looking to the future. Instead the man she loved despised her. Add to that her guilt over the damage she'd done to Ryan and his family, her financial challenges and the loss of her store. Her will to fight was gone. She might as well give up and return to Greenville.

"I'm happy for you both," Zoe said. "Harrison is a great guy and he deserves to be with someone wonderful."

"I don't know that I necessarily fit the bill." London's expression twisted with remorse. "We've done a terrible thing."

"I know," Zoe admitted. "I really regret meeting Everly and agreeing to go after Ryan."

"So do I." London's voice dipped into ominous tones. "I think she's crazy."

Zoe nodded. "And dangerous. She told Tristan what we're up to."

London looked more annoyed than surprised. "She sent Harrison a recording of me saying that I'd used

Harrison as a way to get to Tristan and that Harrison meant nothing to me. I was trying to conceal from her that I'd fallen in love with him and he took my words at face value."

The video of Jefferson and Patty Joyce flashed in Zoe's mind. "What happened?"

"I told him everything and miraculously we're still together."

"I'm glad," Zoe said, recalling her own stab at telling Ryan the truth.

"I'm really lucky he did. When trust leaves a relationship, it's a hard thing to regain."

"And sometimes you never can."

Despair consumed Zoe without warning. The pain of it struck fast and hard, doubling her over. She buried her face in her hands as hot tears filled her eyes. A gentle hand rubbed her back, soothing her.

"It's going to be okay," London murmured. "Whatever you need, Harrison and I will help you."

"No one can help. Everly…" She gulped air into her lungs, shuddering at the effort it took to breathe.

"Let me get you some tea and then you can tell me all about it."

London set a box of tissues on the coffee table within Zoe's reach and headed out of the room. With her bout of hysteria fading, Zoe wiped her eyes and blew her nose.

"Here you go," London said, setting down a tray containing two steaming bone-china cups, crystal sugar and creamer containers, and cloth napkins. "It's Lavender Earl Grey."

While Zoe added a splash of cream to her cup, London departed, returning a minute later with a plate of cookies and several strawberries.

The impromptu feast made Zoe smile. "You sure know how to throw a party," she murmured, nibbling on a shortbread cookie.

"It is what I do for a living, after all," London pointed out. "Are you feeling better?"

"Much. Tea and sugar helps," Zoe said. "Thank you." To her dismay a fresh wash of tears filled her eyes. "Oh, damn." She dabbed at her eyes with a tissue. "I'm not usually like this, but it's just been a terrible day."

"Earlier you said it's so much worse than I knew," London said. "What has been going on?"

Zoe went into detail about her financial difficulties because of the divorce and how they'd affected her store. How Ryan and Susannah had helped. She explained about the video and that Ryan was on his way to break the news to his sister.

"Susannah was so wonderful," Zoe finished. "I couldn't bring myself to do anything bad to her or the campaign, but in the long run it didn't matter. Everly took matters into her own hands."

"I know it seems bad," London said, "but I can't imagine that if the affair gets out it's going to cause Susannah any lasting damage. It's not as if she was the one caught cheating. In fact, people might feel bad for her."

"I hope that's the case, but she's still going to be devastated."

"I agree, but it's not because of anything you've done.

Or even what Everly did. Her husband is the one who betrayed her."

"I'm not sure either Ryan or Susannah will see it that way. He's fully blaming me for the mess."

"That's ridiculous."

Whatever else London intended to say was interrupted by a call coming in on Zoe's cell. She frowned at the unfamiliar number.

"Are you going to answer it?" London asked.

"What if it's Everly?" Zoe let the call roll to voice mail and then listened to the message on speaker.

"Zoe, this is Paul Watts. Ryan told me what's going on and I'd like to talk to you about the documents you received from London McCaffrey."

Both women looked up from the phone at the same time and their gazes locked. In London's gaze she saw the same anxiety fluttering in her chest.

"Who is Paul Watts and why is he asking about the documents?"

"He owns a company that specializes in cybersecurity, and is Ryan's best friend."

A very unladylike curse slipped from London's lips, but her expression grew resolute. "Call him back. See if he can come here tonight."

"Are you sure?"

"I think we both need to face up to what we've done," London said. "And if we can take Everly down with us, all the better."

In the three days since Ryan had broken the news to his sister about her husband's infidelity, Susannah had been square in the middle of a media storm. She and Gil had decided to go on the offensive about Jefferson's affair before the video could be leaked and effectively turned the court of public opinion in her favor.

Susannah's campaign had picked up dozens of volunteers and the inflow of donations had skyrocketed. As far as her run for state senate went, Zoe and her friends had actually helped his sister. Personally, however, Susannah had been dealt a significant blow.

Ryan trotted up the stairs to his sister's house, noting the darkness lurking behind the French doors that opened up onto the wraparound deck. The air of emptiness was unusual for a house that was usually blazing with light. With his uneasiness increasing, he rang the bell and barely heard the chime ring over the cacophony of insect noises.

The home sat on two acres and backed up to deepwater access just minutes from Charleston Harbor. Jefferson was an avid boater and loved to spend the weekends on the water with his kids. Susannah preferred to keep her feet on solid ground and didn't usually accompany them on their adventures.

On the other side of the glass door a figure came toward him through the darkness. Ryan recognized Susannah's housekeeper by her petite frame.

Candi opened the door and scowled at him. "It's late."

Ryan ignored the rebuff. "How is she doing?"

"How do you think she's doing?" Candi had been with the Kirby family since Susannah and Jeff had married. She was an integral part of the household and fiercely loyal to Susannah.

"Can I come in and talk to her?"

With a disgusted snort, Candi stepped back and gestured him inside. "She's on the dock."

That caught Ryan by surprise. He would've expected to find his twin in the place she was most comfortable: her home office. "What is she doing out there?"

Candi glared at him. "She's a grown woman, not a child for me to check on."

Throwing up his hands in surrender, Ryan cruised into the kitchen for a beer before heading out the French doors leading from the kitchen to a set of stairs down to the yard. From the back steps to the end of the dock, it was the length of a city block. With each stride Ryan's heart hammered harder and harder as he contemplated what sort of state his sister was in.

Although she had to hear his footsteps on the wood dock, she didn't shift her gaze away from the moonlit water as he slid onto the Adirondack chair beside hers. A half-empty bottle of bourbon sat near her feet and she was swirling liquid in a crystal tumbler.

Ryan sipped his beer and filled his lungs with the night air while he waited for whatever Susannah felt like sharing.

"Jeff's gone," she said at last. "Just packed a bag and walked out on ten years of marriage."

"Ah, hell, SuSu, I'm sorry."

"You should be," she said dully. "It's all your fault."

The accusation didn't surprise him, but her defeated tone did. It wasn't like his sister to give up.

"If it wasn't for you, my campaign wouldn't be under attack."

Even though Zoe and her friends had caused Susannah's current situation, Ryan recognized his actions had created the problem.

"I'm sorry," he said. "If I hadn't tried to help Kelly Briggs—"

Susannah seemed oblivious to the tears pouring from her eyes and soaking her cheeks. "What am I going to do without him?"

The raw despair in his twin's voice savaged Ryan's heart. He'd never heard anything like this from Susannah. She was the strong, steady one. Now, to hear her sound so despondent, it was as if some fundamental part of her had shattered, never to be repaired.

Ryan reached for her hand and wrapped his fingers around hers. "You can do anything you set your mind to," he told her, squeezing gently. "Fix your marriage. Go on without Jeff. You are our family's greatest success story."

Susannah dashed the back of her free hand across her cheek. Her breath flowed out of her in a ragged hiss. She looked no less beaten, but her fingers pulsed weakly in Ryan's grip.

"My husband cheated. And even though Abernathy didn't get to leak the video, he will use it to attack my worthiness as a state senate candidate. I think most people would point to me as a blistering example of what not to do." She picked up her glass and swallowed the remaining contents in a single gulp. For a long moment she stared out over the water. "Maybe I took too much for granted. My marriage. My career. It was always about what I wanted. What was good for me."

"Don't start blaming yourself. Jefferson had the affair."

"Sure, but did I drive him to it?"

"'Drive him'?" Ryan echoed with a heavy dose of skepticism. "Why? Because you were focused on your career and your family? Because he wasn't your first priority? Don't be ridiculous."

"Nothing this bad has happened to me before." She turned her gaze on him. "I wasn't there for you enough during the Kelly Briggs incident," she said, her fingers tightening fiercely over his. "I'm sorry."

"Don't be." Ryan hated seeing his sister like this. "What can I do to help you? Name it. Anything goes. I can beat the crap out of Jefferson if it would make you feel better. Just say the word."

"I think there's been more than enough payback going on, don't you?" Susannah sighed. "Have you spoken with Zoe?"

"No. Why would I do that?"

"To see how she's handling things."

"Can you really be worried about her after what she did to you?"

"She didn't do anything to me." Susannah frowned at him. "This wasn't her fault. Jefferson cheated. Your actions brought Everly Briggs into our lives."

"Zoe lied to us."

"Not about who she is or how much she cares about you."

Ryan shook his head, vigorously denying Susannah's

claim. "She used me to get to you. That's all there is to it."

"Oh, don't say that. I don't want both of us to lose the people we love over this."

"I don't love her."

"Really? Because you've been acting as if you do." Before he could dispute that, she continued. "I've never seen you this miserable over a breakup before. She hurt you badly and you're busy beating yourself up about how you should've seen it coming."

"Whatever." Ryan hated how well Susannah knew him. "The fact is she lied to me and I can't ever trust her again."

"People make mistakes all the time," his sister said. "The key is to learn from them. I think Zoe has done that. She must feel terrible for what she did to you. Forgive her."

"Are you going to forgive Jefferson?" Ryan countered. "Can you ever trust him again?"

"I don't know yet, but I'm not giving up without trying and neither should you."

Ever since she'd first started Second Chance Treasures, Zoe had kept the store open on Wednesday nights until nine. Labeling the event Girls Night Out, she served glasses of wine and treats to draw in customers and offered crafting or art demonstrations. Some weeks they made as much money in those few hours as they did the balance of the week. Tonight had been no exception.

Too bad it wasn't enough to save the store.

Earlier that day, Zoe had contacted her artists with the terrible news that Second Chance Treasures was closing in less than a month. She'd received responses of sorrow and sympathy with some anger mixed in. Zoe weathered it all with ever-sinking spirits, knowing that she'd failed these women who'd counted on the money they made from selling items in her store.

All through the evening, Zoe had called on reserves she'd never plumbed before and maintained a bright smile. As much fun as the event could be, the long day was draining and with her emotions running high, Zoe was glad when at a little after nine, she headed to the front door to throw the lock.

As she reached the glass door, a figure stepped into the glow of light spilling onto the sidewalk. Zoe's heart plunged as she recognized Ryan's sister, but dreading what Susannah had to say didn't stop Zoe from welcoming her inside.

"Can we talk?" Susannah asked, showing none of the hostility Zoe would've expected.

"Talk?" she countered, locking the door and sealing them in like two combatants in a cage fight. "Or are you here to yell at me for everything that's happened?"

"I don't yell," Susannah replied tartly.

"No, you just shred people with your rhetoric."

The corner of Susannah's mouth kicked up. "While that's more accurate, I'm not here to accuse you of anything. I want to understand."

And Zoe wanted to explain.

"Come into the back," Zoe said, flipping off the light

at the front of the store and gesturing for Susannah to follow her.

Susannah's keen gaze swept over the cot and packing boxes that held her extra inventory. Zoe had shopped at several thrift stores to find furniture pieces, lamps and decorative things to make the space more comfortable, but it was still a storage area in a retail space.

"Are you living here?"

"For another couple weeks and then I'm closing the store and moving to Greenville." Zoe offered no more explanation and Susannah didn't ask any follow-up questions. "Would you like some tea?"

"Do you have anything stronger?"

Zoe shot a glance at Ryan's sister, trying to determine if she was being serious. How much stronger?

"There's lemon vodka in the freezer for emergencies."

"Perfect." Susannah nodded. "Break it out. This is definitely an emergency."

Unsure what the other woman meant, Zoe nevertheless poured shots of vodka over ice and gestured at the small table the staff used for breaks. Since Susannah had been the one who'd initiated the encounter, Zoe decided to let her speak first.

"Tell me about your relationship with Everly Briggs."

Zoe winced. "Relationship is the wrong word. It started with a random encounter at a networking event."

She then went on to lay out their conversation and how they'd arrived at the scheme to take down the three men who'd hurt them. Susannah listened in silence, asking no questions, but her eyes glowed with keen interest.

"It sounds like she played both you and London to get what she wanted," Susannah remarked over an hour later as Zoe's tale wound down.

"You're probably right. We were stupid to get involved with her, but in our defense, we were both in a pretty bad place emotionally and mentally."

During her narrative, Zoe hadn't taken a sip of her drink, but now she swallowed nearly half the shot, closing her eyes as the watered-down liquor burned her throat and warmed her chest enough that the ache around her heart eased somewhat.

Regardless of whether Susannah remained angry, the confession had brought Zoe a modicum of peace. For so long she'd held on to fear, unhappiness, anger and remorse. Being filled with so many negative emotions had kept her from embracing the brighter, lighter feelings from all the good in her life.

Opening the store had inspired a sense of accomplishment and given her a community of women she could trust. Meeting Ryan had awakened hope and given rise to her sexuality in a way she'd never known. Yet full happiness had eluded her because she remained tethered to the revenge bargain she and London had made with Everly.

"I'm really sorry for everything that happened between you and your husband. I had no business going after you as a way to hurt Ryan. It was wrong and I have no way to make any of it up to you."

"I've spent a great deal of time thinking about you these last few days," Susannah said, her gray eyes—so like her twin's—drilling into Zoe with all the force of her significant resolve. "As well as reflecting on my marriage and the choices I've made."

Zoe resisted the urge to squirm as she awaited whatever hell Susannah decided to rain down on her, knowing she deserved everything the lawyer had to say.

"If you'd never showed up in my life, Jefferson would still be cheating. No doubt Abernathy and his dirty tactics would've broken the scandal as a way to muck up the race."

"That's not necessarily true," Zoe said, but she didn't fully believe it.

Susannah shrugged. "Regardless, Everly Briggs would've come after Ryan via my campaign if you'd never been in the picture. From what you've told me, she interfered between London and Harrison Crosby the same way she did by telling your ex-husband what you were up to."

"I suppose you're right." Zoe wasn't sure if she should let herself feel relieved that Susannah was showing mercy.

Since getting to know Susannah, it had bothered Zoe more and more that by betraying Ryan's sister, Zoe had behaved like some of the women in her former social circle.

"If I asked you stay away from my brother, would you?" Susannah's abrupt question wasn't one Zoe had expected, but she should have.

"You don't need to ask." The tightness in Zoe's chest made breathing difficult so the words came out in a wheezy rush. "He made it clear that he doesn't want to have anything more to do with me."

"He's hurt."

A lump formed in Zoe's throat. "I hurt him."

Susannah waggled her glass, setting the ice cubes to tinkling. "I think I could use a refill."

Zoe fetched the bottle and more ice, setting both on the table within Susannah's reach.

"You didn't answer my question," Susannah said. "Would you stay away from my brother?"

Susannah's request wasn't particularly difficult to agree to given Zoe's last conversation with Ryan. "Yes."

"Because I asked or because you're not in love with him?"

"I don't see why it matters. Your brother made it clear how he feels about me."

"It matters because I'm trying to decide whether or not to fight for my marriage and I really need to believe that love can conquer all right now."

"Love…" Zoe mused. "Before Ryan came along, I'd never believed in it. I think you know that my own marriage wasn't based on anything romantic or grounded in respect and trust."

"And now?"

"I love Ryan with all my heart. It's why I couldn't go through with damaging your campaign. You are so important to him that by harming you, I'd be hurting him." Zoe blew out her breath. "I just wish I'd been truthful earlier. Maybe I could've saved all of us a lot of pain."

"Not me," Susannah said, her dry smile one of sorrow but also strength. "I created my heartbreak all by myself."

Silence filled the room for several minutes while Susannah stared off into space, giving Zoe time to contemplate all that had been said. Did Susannah want Zoe to stay away from Ryan? Why not just say that instead of asking if she would?

Could Susannah be okay with Zoe and Ryan being together? More importantly, was it possible that Ryan could someday forgive her? And was she strong enough to fight for his love?

"Why are you closing Second Chance Treasures?" Susannah said, breaking into Zoe's thoughts. "Ryan told me you'd gotten a handle on your financial troubles and that the store was doing better."

"My ex-husband bought the building so he could evict me."

"You could move somewhere else and start over."

"I don't have enough money." Grief welled up in Zoe. She blinked back tears. "And even if there was, I don't have enough fight in me to pick up the pieces."

"So what are you going to do instead?"

"Go back to Greenville and get a job."

"What about all the women you help with the store? If you aren't able to fight for yourself, what about them?"

Zoe's heart gave a painful wrench at Susannah's question, but she set her chin and gestured around the space. "This is all I have. Once I lose it…"

"Let me help you."

Even as Zoe shook her head, she realized she'd underestimated the strength of Susannah's will.

"You can and you will." Susannah's eyes burned with feverish intensity. "Now, why don't you pull out the documents London got from Tristan and let's see what we can do to get you a better settlement."

"I gave everything back to Tristan."

For several seconds Susannah regarded her in surprise. "Can you go after the company who bought the building? Tristan is the owner, correct?"

Zoe brightened. Here was a question she could answer. "TA Charleston Holdings, LLC. But it won't do you any good. It's an offshore company that isn't subject to US laws." She'd done some research.

"Don't be so cynical. I know several very good attorneys who are quite familiar with the ins and outs of offshore tax shelters."

"I don't know if it's worth pursuing," Zoe hedged. While the idea of hitting Tristan where it hurt appealed to her, her instincts cautioned against trying. "You don't know what Tristan is like."

"You're afraid of him."

Zoe nodded. "He scares me more than Everly does."

"Well, neither one of them scares me," Susannah declared and Zoe hoped that wasn't the vodka talking. "You deserve to be treated fairly and I'm willing to play dirty to make that happen."

Twelve

"What brings you by?" Ryan asked, gesturing his sister inside.

"I wanted to talk to you about Zoe."

Ryan's first impulse was to snap at his twin about staying out of his personal life, but he swallowed it. Susannah's concerned expression told him she was trying to help.

"What about Zoe?"

"I went by the store to see her."

He led the way into his living room and turned off the TV. As silence pressed down on the space, he exhaled heavily.

"Why did you do that?"

Susannah sat on his couch, looking unruffled at his grouchy attitude. "I wanted to hear her version of what happened with Everly Briggs."

"And now that you have?"

"She regrets ever meeting the woman and wishes she could change the decisions she made."

"Don't we all." Ryan flopped onto the couch and leaned his head back against the cushion beside his sister. "Have you spoken with Jefferson?"

"Of course." Susannah sounded surprised at his question.

"And?"

"And what?"

"Are you getting a divorce?"

"It's far too early to make such a decision. He's ended the thing with Patty." Susannah's even tone gave no indication how she felt about that.

Ryan's heart ached for his sister. "I guess that's a start? So, what's next?"

A faint line appeared between Susannah's brows. "I'd like to keep my family intact. We've decided to seek counseling." With a fond smile, Susannah reached out and squeezed his hand. "But what I really wanted to talk about tonight is you and Zoe."

"There is no me and Zoe."

"She's planning to leave Charleston," Susannah said.

This news was a blow Ryan wasn't ready for. "When?"

"As soon as she gets everything settled with the store. She's being evicted."

"Why?"

"Seems her ex-husband bought the property so he could continue to mess up her life." Sympathy glinted in Susannah's eyes.

The news roused his protective instinct. "Why didn't she tell me?"

"She found out the same day she received the video," his sister explained. "Maybe she thought my problem was more important than her own."

Ryan closed his eyes against the sharp pain in his chest. "You can't possibly be taking her side in this, too."

Susannah waved away his accusation. "I'm not taking sides. What do you mean 'too'?"

"Paul thinks I'm crazy to let her go."

"I've always liked Paul. He's very sensible."

"You only like him when he agrees with you."

"That's not true." Susannah grinned. "I had a huge crush on him in high school. We even dated for a month."

"You what?" Ryan couldn't believe what he was hearing. "When?"

"Spring of senior year." Susannah's eyes twinkled. Actually twinkled. "We decided you wouldn't like it so we kept our relationship a secret from you." While Ryan tried to wrap his head around his sister and best friend dating, Susannah continued. "Do you hate me? Or Paul? Are we less trustworthy because we kept something from you all these years?"

Ryan saw right away where she was going. "Of course not," he snapped, but couldn't ignore a tiny blip of discomfort. The feeling faded quickly, but there was no denying that his perception of Susannah and Paul had altered minutely. "And what Zoe did was so much worse."

"Was it? She planned to do something and didn't. In high school Paul and I actively spent a month lying to you and have kept you in the dark ever since." Susannah paused, giving him a moment to absorb her point. "Your relationship with Zoe progressed faster and farther than any before it. You've probably been feeling a bit exposed and insecure, but latching onto her mistake as an excuse to dump her so you avoid getting hurt?" Susannah shook her head. "Not cool, brother."

"I need to think about it."

"Don't think too long. She needs a hero to rescue her from that wretched ex-husband of hers."

"How am I supposed to do that?"

"Paul and I have some ideas how to make that happen." Susannah's expression was positively devilish. "And to put an end to Everly's revenge plot once and for all."

Zoe started as a knock sounded on the back door leading out to the parking lot. She wasn't expecting any of her artists to stop by to pick up their inventory and the next person who popped into her mind was Everly. Although she was tempted to ignore the summons, curiosity poked at her and she went to open the door.

"Ryan?" Her lungs seized as she stared at him, buffeted by longing and regret. "What are you doing here?"

"Susannah told me you were closing the store and leaving Charleston."

A lump formed in her throat, preventing her from speaking, so she nodded. He looked so wonderful standing there with his dark hair tousled and his gray eyes somber and concerned. She clenched her hands into fists to keep from throwing herself against his wide chest, wrapping her arms around his neck and sobbing her misery on his strong shoulders.

"Do you want to come in?"

"Thanks."

The instant he stepped across the threshold, she knew she'd made a mistake. Overwhelming despair swamped her, bringing tears to her eyes.

"I'm so sorry," she murmured, turning away. She dashed moisture from her cheeks, but it was just as swiftly replaced with new tears.

"Zoe."

It was just her name, but the throb of emotion in Ryan's voice sent her anguish spiraling ever deeper. Over the last year she'd spent way too much time pondering all the poor choices she'd made. Yet, the entire list of regrets didn't equal her remorse over what she'd done to lose Ryan's trust.

When his hands closed over her upper arms, she covered her face with her hands and nearly doubled over as raw pain bloomed in her chest. She wished he wasn't being so kind. His anger she could face without breaking down, but his compassion twisted her inside out.

"Ah, sweetheart, don't cry." He pulled her back against his chest and wrapped his arms around her. "I'm sorry."

His apology shocked her into laughter. "Why?"

Ryan spun her around and wiped her tears away with his thumbs. "Because I overreacted when you told me what you'd been up to."

She gulped in several ragged breaths before she could speak. "You didn't."

"Everyone disagrees with you." He pulled her back into his arms and set his cheek against the top of her head.

Zoe resisted his warm embrace. She couldn't reconcile how angry he'd been at their last meeting with this loving, forgiving man. What had transformed his attitude in the days since she'd shown him the video? Zoe knew Susannah had gone public with Jefferson's affair, and that must've taken a toll on the entire family. Yet Ryan's twin had graciously reached out to Zoe. And forgiven her. Why did she believe Ryan would do anything less?

Because her perceptions of Ryan had been poisoned by Everly describing him as vindictive when crossed.

"I'm so sorry," she repeated again. Surrendering to her heart's desire Zoe wrapped her arms around his waist and held on tight.

"Let's be done with all the apologizing. I forgive you. If you can forgive me, then we can get past this and move forward with our lives."

She wasn't surprised he wanted closure on their relationship. He wasn't the sort who left things undone.

"Okay."

Relief mixed with disappointment as Zoe pressed her cheek against his thudding heart. If they weren't meant to be together, at least she could find peace in a warm parting, released from guilt and able to recall their time together free from shadows.

"Good." Ryan's gave her a squeeze before easing away. "Now, I have something for you."

While Zoe wiped away the last trace of tears, Ryan pulled an envelope out of his jacket pocket.

"What is that?"

"Open it and see."

Unsure what to make of his eager expression, Zoe opened the flap and peered inside. She glimpsed some sort of legal documents and frowned.

"Are you suing me?"

Ryan's eyes went wide and for a long moment he appeared too stunned to speak. Then his breath hissed out and he shook his head.

"Damn, you've really been through the wringer, haven't you?" He took the envelope back and pulled out the pages, turning them so she could read what was written. "You are now the proud owner of this building."

Unable to process what she was hearing, Zoe stared at the document. "But Tristan owns the building."

"Not anymore. For the sum of ten dollars, he sold it to you."

The news jolted her, giving rise to hope. "Why would he do that?"

"Let's just say that Paul, Susannah and I can be very persuasive when we combine our talents."

"You did this?" Zoe shifted her gaze to Ryan. "Why would you help me after everything…?"

"I needed a way to keep you around." He put the papers back in the envelope and dropped them on a nearby box before taking her hands in his.

"You do?" Zoe's heart began to race at the expression on his face. "But you said we should move forward with our lives."

"Damn it, Zoe." He dropped his chin to his chest and shook his head. "I meant together."

A strange buzzing filled her ears as she gazed up into Ryan's gray eyes and drank in the open affection with which he stared down at her. Her mind was slow to accept what she was seeing. Could he really want to be with her after everything she'd done?

"Oh."

"'Oh'?" he echoed, his tone wry. "Is that a yes?"

Yes. Yes. Yes! The word blasted through her mind, but she'd been through so much in the last year. It seemed impossible that everything had worked out so perfectly for her.

"Are you sure?" she asked, wanting so desperately for him to reassure her, but terrified that he might change his mind after further thought.

His eyebrow rose. "Do you still love me?"

"Of course," she shot back, a smile trembling on her lips even as her throat tightened. "Always and forever."

"That's exactly how I feel about you." His smile lit up her entire world. "I love you so much. You're the best thing that's ever happened to me and I want to spend the rest of my life with you."

This perfect moment seemed too fragile to last. Zoe needed a few seconds to linger in the perfect bliss of Ryan's declaration. While her gaze toured his handsome face, she let her past hurts and failures fall away. Those things no longer had power over the Zoe Alston reflected in Ryan's eyes.

He saw her as good and strong and worthy. Basking in his admiration, she felt beautiful both inside and out.

"I want that, too," she whispered, her confidence skyrocketing.

This man had seen her at her worst and found a way to love her despite all her flaws. He'd accepted that she wasn't perfect and had never required her to be anything other than who she was. They'd weathered her mistakes and she trusted that their love would carry them through any crisis.

That was more than enough to build a future on and Zoe couldn't wait to begin.

Epilogue

At a little after three thirty in the afternoon, Everly entered Connor Properties and stepped up to the receptionist desk. "Everly Briggs to see Devon Connor."

The pretty brunette smiled and said, "Have a seat. I'll let Gregg know you've arrived."

Ten minutes later, a slender man in his midtwenties entered the lobby and headed in her direction.

Gregg's smile was cool as he approached. "Hello, Everly. How nice to see you're early." No doubt Devon's assistant was referring to a meeting a couple of weeks earlier when she'd stood Devon up. "I'll take you to the conference room so you can get set up."

"Thank you," she said, scowling at Gregg's back as she followed him down the hall.

She'd been to Connor Properties several times since

she'd pitched her branding approach to Devon three years earlier. Since then he'd doubled the number of resorts he owned and his account had grown to the point where it was over two-thirds of her business.

"Right in here." Gregg ushered her into a conference room. "Can I get you anything? A cup of coffee? Some bottled water?"

"I'm fine."

After showing her how to connect her laptop to the projector, Gregg left Everly to set up her presentation. In addition to the new design for the website, she had mocked up some brochures and promotional materials. Everly hoped Devon liked this version. He'd been very disappointed with the last two concepts she'd presented and if this round went badly, she might lose all his business.

The conference room door opened and Everly looked up. Delight coursed along her nerve endings as Devon Connor entered the room. Not only was he a brilliant businessman, but also one of Charleston's most eligible bachelors and Everly had long wished they had more than a professional relationship. However, her heart stopped a second later as she spied the pair who came into the room behind him.

"Good afternoon, Everly," Devon said.

Usually his deep voice gave her butterflies. Today all she felt was nauseated.

"Hello, Devon." Although she greeted him, her eyes were drawn to his companions. "What's going on?"

"These two were interested in speaking with you before our meeting." He arched one dark eyebrow at her. "That's not a problem, is it?"

"No, of course not." She swallowed hard and forced a smile.

"Wonderful. I'll be back in fifteen minutes." With that, he exited the room, abandoning Everly to her fate.

"What the hell are you doing here?"

London raised her eyebrows at Everly's tone. "Being blindsided isn't a lot of fun, is it?"

"We regret our part in plotting against Linc, Tristan and Ryan," Zoe piped up. "It was wrong."

"People were hurt." The event planner looked cool and composed in an exquisite sky-blue suit and triple string of pearls. "Ourselves included, and we want you to stop."

"Stop? Why would I do that? You both betrayed me." Everly glared from London to Zoe. "You two deserve everything that happened to you and so much more."

"You have to stop," Zoe exclaimed, glancing to London for support.

From the start Everly had pegged her as the weak link and sent her next words into the heart of Zoe's fears. "I don't have to do anything of the sort. And you forget I have an ally in this little game we've all been playing. Have you forgotten what you tried to do to Tristan?"

"What she tried to do?" London countered. "You disclosed that Zoe had targeted him. He went after her store."

Everly hadn't heard that. She smiled in satisfaction. "Good."

"No," Zoe shot back. "It's not good. All the revenge and payback has to stop."

"We're going to stop you."

There was no way Everly was going to let these two tell her what she had to do. "And how do you plan to do that?"

As she spoke, the conference room door opened again. Everly composed her face, expecting to see Devon Connor, but the four people who walked in shocked her to her toes.

Susannah Dailey-Kirby entered first, her beautiful face lit with satisfaction at Everly's surprise. She was followed by her brother, who stopped behind Zoe. From their body language, Everly guessed the break-up rumors were wrong. Harrison Crosby was there, as well, lending London his support.

Rounding out the quartet was Paul Watts, Ryan's best friend. Everly wasn't sure whether he or Susannah presented the most danger, but suddenly she wasn't feeling all that steady.

"I don't know what you all think you're doing here," she declared, deciding to go on the offensive. "But I won't be intimidated."

"Oh, I think you will," Susannah Dailey-Kirby replied smoothly.

"Your little vengeance plot stops here and now," her brother put in, his expression like granite.

Everly crossed her arms over her chest. "Or what?"

Ryan Dailey scowled. "Or we'll ruin you."

There was a reason they'd chosen to confront her at Connor Properties. Meeting here delivered a strong message. If she didn't agree to their terms, they would mess with her business. Well, she wouldn't be strong-armed like that.

"I'll take you all down with me."

"And who do you think the world will believe?" Zoe demanded, showing more backbone than she ever had before. "All of us or you?"

"In addition, I have a statement from the hacker you hired to get into Tristan Crosby's computer," Paul Watts said.

"But I didn't use the flash drive," Everly protested, pointing at London. "You did."

The event planner shook her head. "Wrong again."

Everly did not like how this was going. She hadn't been able to get justice or revenge for Kelly. Neither Linc nor Ryan had been punished. And London had fallen in love with Harrison. Nothing had gone according to plan and she seemed to be the only one paying a price.

"So are you going to give up and leave us in peace?" Zoe asked, her voice softening.

The sympathy in her gaze was almost more than Everly could bear. "I hate all of you," she snarled.

"But you'll leave us alone," London persisted.

"We don't want to hurt you," Zoe said. "We just want all this to end."

A coalition of six determined people stared at her, awaiting her answer. Everly was out of trump cards and dirty moves. Despite what Zoe had said about not wanting to hurt her, Everly knew if she persisted, they would do whatever it took to make her pay.

Still, seeing London and Zoe so happy, while her sister rotted in jail, made her more resolved than ever to fight. At least that was her plan until the door opened and Devon Connor appeared. His attention went straight to her and something in his unrelenting stare warned her he knew more than he'd let on.

"Have you settled everything?" he asked.

"Not quite," Susannah said. "But I think Everly was just about to agree to our terms."

Rage rose in her. She didn't want to give up or to give in, but with Devon's keen blue eyes watching her intently, Everly recognized she had to stop her vendetta or risk losing her business.

"Fine," she snapped, unsure whom she hated more, the six of them or herself for failing. "Negotiations are over. You win."

"Whew." Zoe blew out her breath as they exited Connor Properties, giddy at being free of Everly and her stupid revenge plot. "That was intense."

The late November sun warmed her face and a light breeze brought the distant chime of a church bell. She linked arms with London, basking in their camaraderie.

"You know," London said, "I almost feel sorry for her."

"Don't you dare," Susannah scolded, coming up on Zoe's other side. "She's responsible for so much heartache. Frankly, I think we let her off too lightly."

Over the last few days Zoe's life had changed in ways she'd never imagined. Not only had she and Ryan made their way back to each other, but now she also had a group of friends she trusted. Starting today, she could stop fretting about what Tristan or Everly might be plotting to do next and start to focus on all the wonderful possibilities her future held.

"Where are we going to celebrate?" Harrison asked as the six of them reached the parking lot.

Paul was the first to shake his head. "Rain check. I'm in the middle of several investigations."

Ryan rolled his eyes at his friend. "When aren't you?"

With a shrug and a wave, Paul headed for his Land Rover.

Zoe watched him go before turning to Susannah. "What about you?"

"Jefferson and I have a counseling session in an hour. I want to swing by the campaign office and let Gil know how this went today." She gave Zoe a quick, hard hug. "You four have fun."

Zoe suggested the rooftop bar at the Vendue and fifteen minutes later they were seated at a table with great views of historic downtown Charleston and the Cooper River. They'd just finished ordering a round of cocktails when Zoe noticed the large diamond sparkling on London's left hand.

"Are you two engaged?" Zoe asked, grabbing her friend's hand and inspecting the engagement ring.

"It must seem fast," London said even as she beamed at Harrison.

"I'm a race car driver," Harrison countered. "Fast is what I do."

"What about you two?" London countered slyly.

Ryan grinned. "I haven't asked her yet."

Yet?

The ink was barely dry on her divorce. It was too soon to think about getting married again. Wasn't it? Zoe's heart skipped at the way Ryan was gazing at her.

"It's been less than a month," Zoe protested but her objection lacked strength.

"Well, what are you waiting for?" Harrison asked.

Ryan pulled something out of his pocket. "I wanted the whole revenge plot problem behind us." He scowled at their companions. "And a little privacy. But after what we've all been through together, maybe it's right that you two are here."

"What are you talking about?" Zoe clapped her hands over her mouth as Ryan slipped from his chair and knelt beside her. "Ryan…" His name escaped her on a low moan.

"Zoe Alston, woman that I love." He paused to grin at her and then, with a dramatic flourish, he popped open the box in his hand. "Will you marry me?"

Zoe's gaze remained locked on Ryan's face as she nodded. Her heart was pounding so hard she thought it might break out of her chest. Never had she imagined it was possible to be this happy.

"Yes. Oh, yes." She leaned forward and wrapped her arms around his neck. "I love you so much."

And then they were kissing and Ryan was sliding the ring on her finger while London and Harrison showered them with congratulations. A bottle of champagne appeared at their table with four glasses so they could toast to love, engagements and the future.

While the men talked football and car racing, Zoe held Ryan's hand and noticed London's fingers were also linked with Harrison's. Luck, fate or some sort of miracle had transformed something that had started so wrong to end so right.

Catching her eye, London leaned in and surprised Zoe by whispering, "I never imagined I could be this happy."

Zoe's throat tightened at the catch in London's voice and she nodded her agreement. "It's pretty amazing how wonderful I feel right now, too."

As she spoke, Zoe caught London's hand, connecting the two couples while the sky darkened above the rooftops of historic Charleston.

* * * * *

If you loved Ryan and Zoe's story,
don't miss the next installment of
Sweet Tea and Scandal
by Cat Schield
coming September 2019
from Harlequin Desire.

Get 4 FREE REWARDS!

We'll send you 2 FREE Books plus 2 FREE Mystery Gifts.

Harlequin® Desire books feature heroes who have it all: wealth, status, incredible good looks... everything but the right woman.

FREE
Value Over
$20

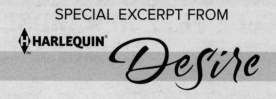
My motto as a woman has always been simple: own
every room you enter. This morning, when I walk into
the offices of Cupid's Arrow, coffee in one hand and
portfolio in the other, the click of my scarlet heels on
the linoleum floor is sure to turn more than a few sleepy
heads. My employees look up from their desks with
nervous smiles. They know that on days like this I'm
raring to go.

Though it sounds bigheaded, I know my ideas are
always the best. There's a reason Cupid's Arrow swept
me up at age twenty. There's a reason I'm the head of
the department. I carry the design team entirely on my
own back, and I deserve recognition for it.

The office doors swing open to reveal Alastair
Walker—the CEO, and the one person I answer to
around here.

"How's the morning slug going, my dear Alexandra?" he asks in that British accent he hasn't quite been able to shake off, even after living in Chicago for a decade. He's adjusting his sharp suit as he saunters into the room. For his age, he's a particularly handsome man, his gray hair and the soft creases of his face doing little to steal the limelight from his tanned skin and toned body.

At the sight of him, my coworkers quickly ease back.

"The slug is moving sluggishly, you might say," I admit, smiling in greeting.

When Alastair walks in, everyone in the room stands up straighter. I'm glad my team knows how to behave themselves when the boss of the boss is around. But my own smile falters when I notice the tall, dark-haired man falling into step beside Alastair.

A young man.

A very hot man.

He's in a crisp charcoal suit, haphazardly knotted red tie and gorgeous designer shoes, with recklessly disheveled hair and scruff along his jaw.

Our gazes meet. My mouth dries up.

And it's like the whole room shifts on its axis.

I head to my private office in the back and exhale, wondering why that sexy, coddled playboy is pushing buttons I was never really aware of before. Until now.

Don't miss what happens when Kit becomes the boss!
Boss
by Katy Evans.

Available March 2019 wherever
Harlequin® Desire books and ebooks are sold.

www.Harlequin.com

HDEXP0219

Want to give in to temptation with
steamy tales of irresistible desire?

Check out **Harlequin® Presents®**,
Harlequin® Desire and
Harlequin® Kimani™ Romance books!

New books available every month!

CONNECT WITH US AT:

Facebook.com/groups/HarlequinConnection

 Facebook.com/HarlequinBooks

 Twitter.com/HarlequinBooks

 Instagram.com/HarlequinBooks

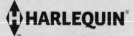 Pinterest.com/HarlequinBooks

ReaderService.com

H HARLEQUIN®
™

**ROMANCE WHEN
YOU NEED IT**

PGENRE2018